WHO SAID CRIME PAYS?

BY

BRYAN FRANKS

Front and back page pictures produced by

Janet Kubala a wonderful friend and lady

Officers in front of Old Gate Lodge going from left to right

Neil Grundy, Stuart McDermott, Wayne Fielding, Alan Blocksidge O.B.E., Tom Brophy and Mick Armstrong
A thank you for your assistance gentlemen.
Also to Natalie Weir thanks for your help, such a lovely lady.

First and foremost I would like to thank my family for being so patience with me and listening to me babble on and on, I love you.
Particularly my wife, lover and soul mate Ann Marie without whom none of this would be possible, I only wish I could give you everything that you deserve, but all I have is my unequivocal love for you.

I have had the pleasure of working with men and women, who I respect, admire and also hold in great esteem, keep up the good work.

Bryan Franks has asserted his right under the Copyright, Designs and Patents Act 1988 to be identified as the author of this book.
This book is a work of fiction, Names and characters are the product of the author's imagination and any resemblance to actual persons, living or dead is entirely coincidental.

I would also like to express my gratitude to the many members of the Prison Service who do a wonderful job and get no thanks or better thought of by the public, this is to tell you that you do make a difference.

"Who said crime pays?"

Bryan Franks is aged 54 he spent just over thirteen years in the Royal Air Force and reached the rank of Corporal.
At 30 he joined Her Majesties Prison Service and has been employed at HMP Parkhurst, Wandsworth, Swaleside, Stocken, Lancaster Farms and HMP Manchester also known as Strangeways (this was where the notorious riot was in the 1990's). He is married to Ann Marie and has been for over twenty years and they have four children and two dogs. He enjoys reading and has been a budding writer for many years but this is the first book that he has attempted to get published.

The main character in this tale is Martin, a prison officer of many years service who is given information that leads to intrigue, danger and a fight for truth and justice. With his band of like minded colleagues Martin uses his new found influence to corrupt, manipulate and bring about change in a system he believes is failing to secure justice for criminal actions.

They call themselves the Brotherhood of the Maahes and the reason behind this is that the
Maahes so myths says was the protector or guardian of Ra the god of the sun disk he was also described as the executioner, a protector of the innocent a guardian of sacred places, or as one who could find "truth".

Prologue

Martin McKay

Aged fifty a hefty built individual, Martin was ex-Royal Air Force and had been involved in the Ireland and Falklands conflicts carrying out all of his duties on the front line, he had travelled all over the world with a Tactical force that had been specially trained to carry out covert operations, whilst in Ireland he would travel round in an old banged up mini looking for unofficial road blocks and then radio them in so that the teams could pounce on and take out the perpetrators of these road blocks, he had a uncanny knack of being able to pick up accents quickly and whilst in Ireland this had helped him get out of some sticky situations.

In the Falklands he was part of the forward site in that theatre of operation directing troops to enemy forces and plotting out and lighting up targets for the bombing runs for the Vulcan bombers, he was returned to England on compassionate grounds when his father was killed by a fellow worker, he had told his dad to use welding rods made of cadmium in a confined space, thus destroying his lungs due to him breathing in the fumes, Martin's dad died an agonising death because of cadmium poisoning his whole body rejected him, his lungs turned to crap and his weight plummeted to nothing and then towards the end it affected his mind.

The guy who caused all of this anguish got of with a light sentence, due to lack of evidence and the fact that someone had deliberately misplaced or destroyed the evidence.

At the age of 30 Martin left the Royal Air Force and joined the Prison Service where he became some years later, the head of the Brotherhood of the Maahes.

PREFACE

Bury Castle was a medieval moated site of possibly 14th century origin. Around 1470 it was strengthened into a fortified manor house, from the 12th Century the de Bury family held a manor here. In 1865 new sewers were constructed in Castle Square and a number of poor brick structures were demolished. An antiquarian called Hardwick observed the sewer and undertook some excavation himself to record the remains of the castle. Hardwick also discovered that beneath this Fortress lay the remains of secret rooms and passages these he kept secret and only a select few would ever know of it whereabouts and more importantly how to access these catacombs.

A century later information about the catacombs came to light via a prisoner, whose death was imminent, he confided the secret to a Prison Officer, a man whom he had befriended during his incarceration. The catacombs were soon to become a meeting place for a band of brothers known as the 'Maahes'[1] one of whom was the Officer. These gentlemen believed they were the saviours of the 'victims', victims who the Courts and the legal system appeared to have let down. They rebelled against the injustice of such a system reeking revenge and justice in a system that was unjust………..

1. Maahes so myths says was the protector or guardian of Ra the god of the sun disk he was also described as the executioner, a protector of the innocent a guardian of sacred places, or as one who could find "truth"

HMP PATRICROFT

HMP Patricroft is a Category "B" core local prison serving the courts within the Manchester area and also assisting prisoners address their offending behaviour, providing courses as well as education facilities.

The establishment held approximately 1,400 prisoners ranging from category "A" (but only the minor end of the category A prisoners, no Exceptional or High risk category A prisoners) to category "C" and those on trial, remand or awaiting sentencing.

There are eight wings within the prison going from A wing to H wing each holding 160 prisoners and a segregation unit whose capacity fluctuated daily depending on the clientele and a V.P. (Vulnerable prisoners) wing which housed 120 of the countries worst criminal offenders. These were sex offenders who had either committed offences against adults, male as well as female, and the one's who had committed offences against children. Also on this wing were prisoners who had requested protection from the mainstream prisoners due to debt, drugs or gang affiliated trouble.

Then there was the category "A" unit which housed those prisoners on the escape list known as E List prisoners as well as the standard category "A" prisoners, (prisoner whose escape would be highly dangerous to the public or the security of the State.)

The offences of the prisoners at this establishment varied from petty criminals up to the more serious crimes such as rape, murder, drug smuggling, drug dealing, armed robbery and so on, they also held prisoners who are on accumulated visits and those for local release who were coming to the end of there sentence.

They kept a number of prisoners for employment within the prison which required a more stable kind of prisoner i.e. kitchen workers, wing cleaners etc.

These kind of prisoners could be reasonably trusted to carry out tasks with the minimum of supervision, it didn't mean that you could just leave them to their own devices because as sure as eggs is eggs these little darlings would rob and steal you blind if you let them, so you could trust them to a certain extent but no further.

You did come across the odd exception to this rule and these prisoners were few and far between unfortunately, one such prisoner was old Charlie Rogers

Chapter 1

It was all quiet on "G" wing; the prison was on a lock down due to a full roll check going on, these were called every now and then by the Governor in charge so that every prisoner in the Establishment could be accounted for. If the numbers didn't tally as they nearly always tended to do, then staff had to carry out a physical check of each cell and then give their wing roll in again to the Centre so that they could coordinate the numbers for the prison.

One of the young officers on G wing was on the fours checking the cells and counting how many were in each one as he went along, when he got to G4-16 he opened the flap and looked in, he suddenly shot back in shock,

"Staff, Staff he shouted, for God's sake get up here I need help,"

The senior officer or S.O. and one of the more senior members of staff appeared on the landing,

"What's up?"

"He's died, Shit he's hung himself, please I can't go in there please," the young officer looked close to tears,

"Quiet down lad, its ok get yourself down the stairs and ring the communications room and tell them what's happened.

Tell them we need medical assistance urgently, plus a blue light", the S.O. opened the flap a bit further so he could see

inside; at the same time he had slipped his key into the lock and was opening the cell door.

The other officer behind him cleared his throat; the S.O. turned and told him,

"You support the body while I cut him down",

They entered the cell, at the same time the young officer got to the office on the Two's.

No-one noticed Alan slipping through the gates on the fours and going across to H wing where he worked.

Alan picked the phone up and called Martin,

"It's done, Dave left first and I made sure he was clear before I left, no-one saw us",

"Good" replied Martin, "now make sure people see you, shout down your numbers, I'll see you later," they both hung up, doing as Martin had said Alan made his presence felt,

"Twenty eight on the fours he shouted to the office below him,"

"That's right" said the desk officer," you sure took your time"

"Just making sure the numbers were correct before letting you know,"

"Kettles on" he shouted back "it's your turn to brew",

"Ok but it's your coffee this time,"

Alan made his way down to the office slowly, looking across to G wing as he did to see if anyone had clocked him, no-one had, he needn't have worried himself, as they were all too busy counting their own wings to be distracted by anyone else.

Hotel 1, the duty medical officer turned up it was A.J. he walked into the cell and checked the prisoner's vitals,

"He's gone" he said glancing at the S.O.

"Damn more paperwork,"

"You and me both" said A.J.

Chapter 2

It was late 1990 and Martin McKay was the Senior Officer in charge of "G wing he was aged fifty a hefty built individual, Martin was ex-Royal Air Force and had been involved in the Ireland and Falklands conflicts carrying out all of his duties on the front line, he had travelled all over the world with a Tactical force that had been specially trained to carry out covert operations, whilst in Ireland he would travel round in an old banged up mini looking for unofficial road blocks and then radio them in so that the teams could pounce on and take out the perpetrators of these road blocks, he had a uncanny knack of being able to pick up accents quickly and whilst in Ireland this had helped him get out of some sticky situations.

In the Falklands he was part of the forward site in that theatre of operation directing troops to enemy forces and plotting out and lighting up targets for the bombing runs for the Vulcan bombers, he was returned to England on compassionate grounds when his father was killed by a fellow worker, he had told his dad to use welding rods made of cadmium in a confined space, thus destroying his lungs due to him breathing in the fumes, Martin's dad died an agonising death because of cadmium poisoning his whole body rejected him, his lungs turned to crap and his weight plummeted to nothing and then towards the end it affected his mind, but the guy who had caused all of this anguish got of with a light sentence due to lack of evidence, and also due to the fact that someone had deliberately misplaced or destroyed the evidence.

At the age of 30 he left the Royal Air Force and joined the Prison Service.

Martin enjoyed working on G wing because everyday was different due to the fact that his was the induction wing for all new prisoners coming into the jail, it held approximately 148 prisoners, some of which were workers on the unit and they had been there for some time, one in particular a prisoner called Charlie Rogers JB1221 had been there for years as the number one cleaner. He was dying of cancer and had refused to go to the Hospital wing as he wanted to stay, as he put it, in his home (G wing). The wing staff knew about his situation and all had agreed that they would keep him and assist him by covering his Hospital appointments if needed. Charlie was coming to the end of his time now and nothing else could be done for him only to make him comfortable, but Charlie being Charlie he was having none of the softly, softly touch he wanted to be treated the same as before, this was so the other prisoners didn't say anything because in his time Charlie was a real handful if he wanted to be and him and the wing S.O. had in the past crossed swords and had done battle, neither had won but both had mutual respect for each other and over the years had become friends in a strange kind of way.

It was around about 15:00 hours when the call for the wing senior officer went over the radio, a few minutes later the S.O. answered,

"What now," he thought to himself don't even get a minutes peace around here, he answered the radio and informed them that he was busy and could be contacted on 5535 in a few moments,"

"Received Alpha 6, I will pass your message on",

The S.O. unlocked the door and walked out onto the one's landing,

"Ok who wants me?" he shouted up to the office,

"It's us", replied the office officer, "old Charlie has asked to see you, he's not well Sir",

"Ok I'm down here anyway I'll go and see him, is that it now can you look after everything else while I sort out old Charlie",

"Yes Sir", the officer replied,

The S.O. turned and walked down the landing towards Charlie's cell, when he got there he looked in,

"Now then you old sod what's the matter with you?" closely followed by,

"My God Charlie you look like, shit",

They both knew that Charlie was nearing the end of his life but that didn't stop the banter between them, why should Charlie being at death's door stop them taking the mickey out of each other, Charlie wouldn't want it any other way.

Charlie had asked to speak to his only friend in the world. Over the years these two had got to know each other very well and old Charlie used to share in the trials and tribulations of the S.O's life outside of the prison. The two of them had a mutual respect for each others situation, Martin understood Charlie's predicament, he was a criminal and as such was only entitled to certain items but on the odd occasion Martin had brought in extra lunch and given it to Charlie, Charlie loved banana's but these were never given because some prisoners smoked the skins and got high.

He made sure that Charlie was employed as a wing cleaner initially and when he started getting worse with the cancer he made sure he was paid even for the days he was unable to work due to the pain, he made him the Wings No1 cleaner but squared it off so that he didn't have to do anything if he didn't want to.

Charlie made sure he was at the servery for every meal time ensuring that the other cleaners and servery workers did their jobs even when he was in agony. They respected this old lag because he had done more bird than they had had hot dinners also with some of them, well most of them, he had been inside before they were born and he was as tough as old boots and had put a stop to many a young pretender wishing to take his title as number one.

"What's up Charlie"? asked the S.O. as Charlie's pad mate left the cell "push the door to Boss" whispered Charlie

"There's no-one around, now what's going on? I've got work to do you know,

"Sorry Martin but this is important to me and could be of some help to you, you know what I'm in for don't you,"

As long as no-one else was around Charlie could call Martin by his first name it was an agreement between the two of them.

"Yes armed robbery and burglaries, you got 25 years and you've nearly done all that",

"That's right boss but the robberies were gold bullion and the burglaries were on financial institutions for bearer bonds, not houses and the reason that they have made me stay in for so long is because they have never recovered a penny from either".

"Listen you have been good to me all these years so I want you to have this",

Charlie passed Martin a piece of paper with a map and a plan drawn on it along with an access code and instructions, Martin looked at Charlie, puzzled.

"What's this for", he said,

"Take it and make sure that you follow the instructions as they are written, do not deviate from them please, promise me",

"I promise",

"Are you in work tomorrow?"

"Yes I'm in tomorrow afternoon",

"I'll see you then and we will talk again once you have seen for yourself",

"Promise me again that you will follow the instructions?"

He looked at Charlie; you could tell he was seriously ill and not long for this world, his gaze softened,

"I will Charlie, I will",

He left Charlie and went off to complete his shift, that night as he was leaving the prison he started to dwell on what Charlie had told him. When he got to his car he sat there for a while until Carney's circus had finished. He could never understand why all the other staff felt the need to drive out of the Prison car park all thinking they were Stirlin Moss.

He removed the piece of paper from his pocket and looked at the map, putting it into his mind, suddenly there was a knock on his window, he nearly jumped out of his skin, when he turned to look it was Terry one of the other S.O's who had just finished, he quickly put the paper away out of sight and wound the window down,

"Love letter" queried Terry,

"Chance would be a fine thing, no such luck it's a shopping list for her indoors",

"Right little lackey, you are!,

"Tell her to get them her self",

"That's why you're on your own mate, you know that you're supposed to be a team and work together, that's what a marriage is",

"Bollocks" he said; as he got into his car and drove off at break neck speed.

Martin wondered about the morality of taking a gift off Charlie, he was after all a con? He shook his head, he didn't even know what it was yet so no point in getting paranoid.

All the way home he kept imagining what was it that Charlie had hidden all those years ago and would it still be there, would it have rotted away to dust or been eaten by rats, it's gold, money, diamonds or maybe even the crown jewels. As he got close to home he remembered that he would need a torch, camera and a holdall, he pulled into his drive and went in shouting as he did so,

"Hi ladies I'm home",

The first to greet him as always were his two Jack Russell's barking at him and jumping up in excitement,

"Ok you guy's calm down", he said, then the dogs ran off barking so as to tell everyone else he was home,

"Dad,"

Came a shout from the living room, he popped his head around the door and there were his four lovely ladies, his wife and his three children,

"Everything Ok at work sweetheart"? said his wife Ann

"Fine, but I have to pop out to Bury Town Centre later, I have an errand to run, is there anything you need while I'm out? "

"No we have everything, tea's in the kitchen I'll just heat it up, you get out of your goon suit and set the table for me and you, the girls have already eaten",

Martin went up stairs and got changed into jeans and a sweatshirt, then went back down and set the table; Ann came in carrying the two plates and placed them down.

They both sat down and began to discuss the day's events, he didn't mention the paper that Charlie had given him but did tell her that Charlie was looking bad, Ann knew about old Charlie and about the cancer.

"Is he in pain, are they looking after him?"

"He's ok but he still won't go on to the Hospital Wing, he says it's like surrendering to the cancer and he's not ready to do that".

I don't think he ever will be, he'll die on the wing in the cell he has had for the last ten years".

After tea he kissed the girls and Ann and left for Bury, it was only a few miles down the road from his house so it didn't take too long getting there.

He pulled into the municipal car park next to the old ruins, got out and paid the car parking fee, returned to his car and took the piece of paper out of his pocket and studied it carefully.

If he was going to chicken out then now was the time, but his curiosity had got the better of him, he now needed to know what old Charlie's secret was.

Martin initially walked around the ruins making sure no-one was waiting for him or watching him, he started eyeing up every nook and cranny to see if anything stood out to him straight away but nothing did.

Maybe the drugs that Charlie was on for his cancer had done his brain in and he was imagining all this, but the map, the access code, the instructions, he was so meticulous and adamant about me following them to the letter, why?

So many questions and no bloody answers, "Stop being a girl and get on with it" he muttered to himself.

Opening the paper and reading the first line it read,

"Facing south look for the Roman sun dial

Once at the sun dial read the inscription on the top"

He looked for the sun dial as he hadn't a clue which way south was, he spotted it in one of the corners so he headed towards it.

He looked at the ornate sun dial trying to understand the Latin writing that was engraved onto the face of the dial.

He read it again, not a hope in hell of understanding this crap he thought, so he took a pen from his pocket and wrote it down, "what a let down this isn't going to be as easy as I thought, I will have to get this interpreted at a later date", he put the piece of paper in his pocket but as he was about to walk away when he noticed the base plate just under the face of the sun dial.

"Who needs a Latin translation the buggers have done it for me thank Christ", he muttered as he began to read it.

Beware the eyes of March,

For they are all around you but only one can see!

"Ok now what do I do now?"

He took out the piece of paper Charlie had given him, just then he heard a noise from behind him, he turned to see a man with his dog walking towards the town centre,

"Jesus Martin you're getting paranoid" he said to himself.

He decided to sit on the bench near by and have a cigarette just so as not to bring any unwanted attention from any passers by.

He walked over to the bench, lit up and then leaned forward to read the paper.

Do as the inscription says and look!

"I bet Charlie's laughing his backside off just imagining me running around Bury like an idiot" he thought.

"No, he wouldn't do that to me, this must be something important to Charlie, I'll keep going, but if this is a mickey take, ill or not he is going to pay".

He started to walk slowly around the ruin walls looking for eyes, that is when he noticed the first one, not very big and not very obvious but there it was and it did look like an eye, but this one was shut, he continued around the walls and every now and again he would spot an eye, then at last he found one that looked like it was open.

He bent down slowly surveying if anyone was watching, looking really close he noticed that in the middle of this particular eye was an indent where the pupil would have been, he pushed it with his finger and the wall popped inward just enough so as not to be so obvious to anyone walking past.

He slowly pushed it until it opened far enough for him to get himself through, once inside he eased the door shut behind him and turned on his torch.

Once his eyes became accustomed to the light he walked forward, that's when he came across his first cobweb one of many that he would encounter on his journey down, he recalled watching a programme which informed the viewers that nobody was more than 7 feet away from a spider at any one time a nice thought if you were arachnophobic lucky for him he wasn't.

The stairs within led you deep underground so that any excavation of the land above for electric's, gas or telephone pipes would not divulge the secret.

He opened the paper up again; he turned the torch towards the paper and then read it aloud to himself"

"Once you get inside, there are numerous escape exits any one of which would bring you out a different point within the town, but these are exists only and there is no access in once the opening has been shut behind. Prior to opening any exit, ensure that the coast is clear by using the spy hole's provided". The stairs at the entrance led down into the depths of the earth or so it felt, at the bottom of the stairs the earth opened up into a large hexagonal shaped room and from four of the points there were tunnels leading off into the dark, there were also three doors, Martin went to the first door and opened it, there were a few steps for him to go down which then brought him onto a level flooring, inside there was a grand table with chairs all around it, it looked like a scene from King Arthur's court at Camelot complete with the round table. He walked over to it and blew some dust and the cobwebs off, "what a beautiful piece of furniture but how did it get down here," he thought as he walked round looking in every corner and checking for any signs or clues that may have been left for him to find, there were none, he turned to walk out and that was when he spotted it.

Behind the door was an alcove and within this alcove was a large gold coloured box with beautiful carvings all over it, Martin walked over to it and slowly inspected all around to ensure that he wasn't going to lose any part of his hands, he'd seen Indiana Jones. On inspecting the outside he noticed what looked like Egyptian hieroglyphics but had no idea what they meant, he took his camera out of his pocket and took a picture, he would check on his computer at home to see if he could decipher the hieroglyphics. He didn't want to take anything because as it stood in his mind he hadn't done anything wrong he was only looking, he made a mental note of the room and it's contents and then moved on to the next room. This one had and alarm system and some kind of key pad access, he remembered that there was an access code written on the piece of paper, so he took it out of his pocket and punched in the numbers, the door opened and again he had to go down a few steps to gain entrance to the room. Once he had stepped down he looked around, this room was more like a store room, there were storage boxes and crates all around the place, walking over to the nearest one he praised off the lid with the crowbar that had been conveniently left on top of it. As the opening widened he looked in, paper wrapped carefully so as to preserve it for years to come, he picked a piece up it was about A4 size and on it was written Bearer Bond the National Bank of America with one hundred thousand dollars written in the top right hand corner of the paper, "holy shit", thought Martin "this must be the mother load".

He stepped back and looked at the size of the crate, this must hold a good hundred or more of these, it was too much for him to comprehend but he knew he was rich, with that thought he wondered what the hell was in the bigger boxes. He rushed over to one of the slimmer boxes and gently opened one end and looked in, this looked like a picture, he pulled the box open so he could see the picture properly, I've seen this before he thought, he always prided himself on knowing a bit about art, strewth this is a Van Gogh "Sunflowers" worth about twenty odd million this has got to be a copy or Old Charlie has stolen it from some art dealer or museum.

He realised he had touched everything and his finger prints were all over this place, he looked around for something to wipe his prints off, he suddenly stopped in his tracks and looked down at his hands.

'Calm yourself you idiot you're wearing gloves', he thought and then slowly lowered the lid laughing quietly to himself and moved onto the next crate. It was another painting but he didn't know this one so he took a picture with his camera. This one was of some ugly looking bird, *'my kid could do a better picture'* he thought to himself, replacing the lid he moved on, the next one was three pictures, *'Don't know this one either'* he muttered and then carried on to the last crate, this was a picture of a guitar or some kind of musical instrument.

After taking photo's of them all including the Sunflowers, he slowly replaced everything back to where it was originally just in case anyone else knew about this place and would know that he had been there.

He walked out of the storeroom and gently closed the door behind him, looking up to the sky he mouthed the words thank you and then moved on to the last of the room, steps again, only this room had shelves with books and trinkets on them, he couldn't imagine old Charlie collecting anything let alone reading all these books, he took more photo's so that he could look at them at his leisure, he didn't want to hang about here any longer than he had to.
He walked out into the antechamber and looked at the four exits tunnels and decided that he would investigate one of them and then come back and check out the others when he had more time.
Before going down the tunnels he decided to check the paper Charlie had given him to make sure that there weren't any more surprises ahead, he read the instructions that Charlie had written and realised that he was not to go down the West tunnel as there could be danger.
'Great," he thought', "which is the West tunnel? "where's a compass when you need one?" who was he kidding that

wouldn't have helped him anyway he was rubbish at North, South, East and West what was he going to do now, he looked up at the tunnel entrances and then noticed the N, S, E and W written above each one, he shook his head and muttered *'For crying out loud Martin you're getting worse, how the hell did you miss those?" 'Right keep clear of West, enie, meanie, minie, mo'*.

That one! He pointed to the North tunnel and with torch in hand he set off.

Using his torch to light up ahead of himself he noticed that there were other tunnels leading off from this one but for the time being he was only going to go straight, the last thing he needed to do was to get lost in this labyrinth, that would take some explaining,

"Oh yes officer this prisoner told me all about these and said I could have them because I was his only friend in the world",

He kept going but then started to wonder how far these damn tunnels went, just then he saw a small chink of light just ahead of him,

"Thank goodness" he thought,

He then began to ascend up some stairs, it was the longest set of stairs he had ever come across, when he reached the top he cleaned of the dust and cob webs off the exit door and looked for the spy hole so that he could check that the coast was clear, he found the spy hole and looked out, there were a few people about at that time but not many, he had a clear view of the whole street but still couldn't work out where in Bury he was,

"Now!" he thought the coast is clear go for it, he released the catch and pushed the door, it swung open and he quickly left ensuring that he closed it behind him securely, he looked around and discovered that he was stood outside the front of the Museum he had exited from one of the large posts either side of the entrance to the building, this was great, but he still had a load of questions for old Charlie.

He gathered his thoughts and made his way back to his vehicle, this was amazing he had walked a good 600 yards away from the entrance to the secret hide away and no-one had noticed anything.

On the way home he had decided not to tell his wife or family anything until he had gotten all the answers from Charlie and even then he wasn't sure if he would because if it was all true and he could do what ever he wanted with the loot.

He started to doubt himself and the morals behind what Charlie had given him access to, would others see this as him taking a bribe, he had been straight all of his life he had and would never do anything underhanded or illegal but this, this would help society and deceit and honest law abiding people feel that they were not alone and someone does care about the hurt and loss that they feel and defend them and make the law breakers pay and also those who chose that path will now pay for their crimes with a better justice system than they currently have," what should I do" thought Martin.

By the time he had made it home he had decided that what he had in mind he didn't want his wife or family involved in as it was illegal and dangerous, "we'll see," he said to himself "first things first".

He went back to old Charlie's cell the following day, when he got to the cell he sent Charlie's pad mate off to the servery, he had already told the cleaning officer that he wanted the landings and the servery cleaning as it was a mess (it wasn't, he just wanted the cleaners well out of his and Charlie's way) he had previously informed the Officer that he wanted the place scrubbed spotless and that he would inspect it before tea was served.

"Right Charlie, "what the hell is going on? "what's all that stuff in your little hidey hole and where did it come from? Is it legal or am I going to get done for aiding and abetting in a crime"?

"Slow down for crying out loud Boss there is no way I would do that to you, everything that you found is legal, fully legit and above board, it's all paid for and the proof of purchases and the authenticity letters from Sotheby's are currently being held for me by a financial colleague",

"Now what you need is the whereabouts of this guy and the password to ensure him that you have been given my permission to have these goods",

"What did you think of the place and the bounty that you found?

"Christ Charlie, are those painting the real McCoy or just copies",

"They're real trust me, they cost me a pretty penny as well, but they were well worth it",

"What about the gold box?" said Martin, "What's inside? I noticed the Egyptian hieroglyphics but decided not to open the box just in case there was a surprise waiting for me,

I'm not Indiana Jones, you know when all those things start to happen like big boulders rolling down on you or your arm gets cut off because you have set off a hidden trap",

Charlie looked at him as though he was from another planet,

"What have you been taking?" asked Charlie, "you have got to get out more and stop watching all of those crazy films, honest boss real life isn't like that, what a vivid imagination you have".

Martin looked at Charlie and started to feel a bit stupid for being so paranoid,

Then he points at Charlie and says "Hey you're the one who started this shit with the "DON'T DEVIATE FROM WHAT'S ON THE PAPER, PROMISE ME PLEASE",

You idiot you had me jumping at every little thing that happened, was this a trap or was that a trap, should I or shouldn't I touch this, for crying out loud, it was like walking on egg shells waiting for something to happen, and all the time imagining you laughing your head off in your cell thinking about me being scared of my own shadow".

Charlie started laughing, looking at Martin and then picturing him trying to remember what he had touched and running round like a headless chicken rubbing prints of anything and everything, he then clutched his chest as his belly laughing made his eyes fill up.

"I wouldn't mind but when I looked at my hand that's when I noticed I had gloves on, this just made Charlie worse, "Oh shut up Charlie and tell me about the stuff in there, how'd you get this stuff and what do you think I will be doing for you?"

Charlie gained control and the laughing subsided, he looked at the S.O. and said,

"In the box is an amulet supposed to have belonged to Maahes and it was thought to protect the wearer from evil and ensure their safe passage in the underworld, great story isn't it, worth a stack so be careful if you are selling it, as to what I want from you, you're doing nothing for me, it's yours to do with as you see fit. It's my gift to you" Martin looked puzzled.

"Look there has got to be millions of pounds worth of art and bearer bonds and other stuff and you're just going to give it all to me and you want nothing in return?"

"Martin you have given me your friendship all these years and you have treated me with dignity and allowed me to gain your trust and respect but if you would, the only thing that I ask for is for you to contact Imee and ask him to give me a decent burial and a headstone the rest is yours".

"Who's the hell is Imee?"

"He's the financial colleague that I told you about, just ask him when you see him to sort out the funeral arrangements and he will do it, and don't concern yourself about Imee he knows which side his breads buttered he will look after you if you need any help shifting the stuff, just be careful he doesn't take more of a cut than he should."

"Now let me give you the low down on Imee so he will know I sent you!"

Chapter 3

Imee's dad Abraham Rosenberg was born in Berlin he was a master jeweller and was renowned throughout the world for his skill and ability, when the second world war broke out the German hierarchy soon learnt to use Abraham's contacts to sell priceless antiquities that they had plundered from the Jews, Museums and the Aristocracy of all the countries that they invaded.

Abraham carried out what the Germans wanted to ensure that he and his family would survive the atrocities that befell other Jews, towards the end of the war Abraham had convinced the two high ranking Germans that he was employed by, Goering and Hess that he needed to go to England to assist with the sale of some of there ill gotten gains, initially they were sceptical about allowing this to happen because Hitler had forbidden any of his people to deal with or collaborate with any Jews and here were two of his top men disobeying him.

Because of their greed they allowed Abraham to go and gave him all the necessary papers that would allow him and his family exit from the country, That was their down fall.

Abraham took the chance and got all of his family out of Germany and across to England safely, he set himself and

Imee up in and shop on Regents Street in London and Abraham then began to teach Imee the trade.

Imee was quick to learn and soon became a Master Jeweller in his own right, but on the side Imee would deal with the criminal underworld to sell their loot to private dealers and collectors and also through his world wide connections he was able to launder gold, monies and bonds.

Abraham's reputation preceded him and not long after setting up shop he was summoned to appear before the boss of MI5.

When Abraham and Imee arrived he was told that Imee would not be allowed into the meeting at this Abraham began to walk away, he was halted by an MI5 agent who asked him to wait for confirmation that his son would be allowed to remain with him.

They were both shown into a large conference room, at one end of the table was gentleman dressed in a Saville row business suit, he had a manila coloured file open in front of him, this contained the immigration paperwork for Abraham and Imee,

"Please sit down gentlemen" he said,

"What's this about? "said Abraham" we have done nothing wrong,"

Imee then thought of all his underhanded dealings with the criminal fraternity, "Oh Christ what have I done? They're going to deport us back to Germany; my whole family will be killed because of me",

"We would like you to do a job for us," stated the well suited gentleman, but this is to remain within this room and if you agree we will accommodate both you and your son until the job has been completed,"

"What job and what do we get from this?

"A hefty lump sum, citizenship and immunity from any prosecution for the rest of your lives, except for capital offences of course."

"Lord! this must be one hell of a job, what do you want us to do steal the crown jewels,"

"Funny you should say that," said the gentleman in the suit

"No way on God's earth are we doing that, you have got the wrong people",

Abraham and Imee stood up to leave but there path was blocked by two burly MI5 agents,

"Wait" said the suited gent, "you haven't heard the full explanation of what we want, please sit down, no-one is stealing the crown jewels, well not on my shift anyway".

Abraham and Imee were shown back to their seats,

"Listen we don't want you to steal the jewels we want you to make replica's of the crown jewels",

"Why in God's name would you want replicas of the crown jewels?"

"Because her Majesty is going to allow them to be shown to the public, which would mean every Tom, Dick or Harriet will be able to get close to them,"

The last time the crown jewels were nearly stolen was in 1671 by Colonel Blood and I can prove I was off that day," laughed the suited man,"

Abraham and Imee didn't laugh so the man coughed and then continued," but the Irish crown jewels were stolen and never recovered, this will never happen to these jewels that is why we require you and your son to make replica's, so that they may be displayed as the originals, do you agree to help us?"

Abraham and Imee both agreed and over the next 3 months they set about making the crown jewels, they were allowed to go home but only after they had be searched and the MI5 agents guarding them were satisfied that they were clean. They were instructed that they were to tell no-one of what they were doing and if anyone found out the deal was off.

Abraham explained to the MI5 man that Imee would be doing the more intricate work as Abraham's sight wasn't what it was but Imee was as good as Abraham if not better, the man explained that they would be given the original crown jewels to sketch from and ensure that even an expert would be fooled, none of these sketches or designs would be allowed out of the building, Abraham had told Imee in secret that they would hide there monogram's somewhere on the jewels so that only those two would know which was real and which was fake and also to ensure that if anything went wrong after the job was over they could expose these people for what they were.

During the time the two of them were making up the crown jewels they would be approached by different MI5 agents and asked if they could make them something special for there loved one's, both Imee and Abraham agreed to make what ever they wanted but insisted that they should be given their real names so as not to get them mixed up with any of the other agents and a contact number so when the job was done they could deliver it to them promptly. None of the agents disagreed with these requests.

Now, whenever a piece of jewellery was completed Imee made sure that the person was on searching that day and would tell them in strictest confidence that he would deliver it to them once they had finished for the day, the agent was to ensure that they searched them because the private piece of jewellery would be in Imee's possession so they were to say nothing when they noticed anything out of the ordinary as it was their jewellery, unbeknown to the MI5 agents and Abraham, Imee was taking out copies of the crown jewels as well, just to make sure he and his father were safe after the job was completed.

When the task was completed Abraham and Imee presented their master pieces to the suited gentleman, he then compared them with the originals and stated that he couldn't tell the difference but he was to seek advice from another jeweller who had full knowledge of the crown jewels and could spot a copy miles away.

The gentleman left and asked the two of them to wait for a few hours until he returned.

Abraham told Imee what and where he had put the monograms on each of the copied items so that in the future if they required it they could use it to there advantage, Imee considered telling Abraham that he had made copies of the crown jewels for the same reason and that they were hidden in their store at Regents Street, but then he thought better of it, Abraham would hit the roof especially if Imee revealed the truth that the jewels in their store were the real crown jewels not copies.

The suited gentleman returned true to his word within two hours, guys these are brilliant my man couldn't tell the two apart, I thank you and so does Her Majesties Government," he lifted a brief case up and placed it on the table and then opened it, inside was two hundred thousand pounds, he spun the case round so that Abraham and Imee could see the contents.

"Also in the case are two cards you are to keep these with you at all times, if for any reason you get into trouble with the Police please show them the card and ask them to call the number on the card, we have had your passports made up for you two and your wife Abraham and you are now all British citizens and under the protection of this Government, once again may I thank you and please remember this is to remain our secret no-one else is to know about this ever is that understood?" both Abraham and Imee nodded.

Imee closed the brief case and the two of them were about to leave when the gentleman in the suit shouted at them to stop.

They turned round Imee knew he'd been caught and was about to own up and throw himself at this mans mercy when the gentleman said, "Ok you two which of these is the real one?" Imee went straight over to him leaving Abraham at the door, "That's the real one" said Imee, pointing to the one on his right side, "That's the fake" pointing to the one on his left, "now can you remember that?," yes" said the gentleman, and then they were gone.

Out on the street Abraham and Imee started laughing like school girls," what a relief that was over, now we have the finance to purchase the shop in Mayfair, that one will be our "Jewel our Crowning Jewel" they said together, they both looked at each other at the same time and started laughing again.

That is the story of Imee and how he and his family became the biggest Jewellers in Britain and how Imee still does a bit on the side for the criminal underworld, but only the select few who knew him previously.

"I have known and dealt with him for years, so we have a professional working relationship and that's it, he won't let you down. You now know all that I know about this man so he will look after you and protect you if you want, so long as it doesn't come on top for him with regard to the police, although he has a get out of jail free card he won't use it unless he has too."

Charlie then went on to explain how to contact Imee and the whereabouts of his businesses in London,

"When you first meet him, introduce yourself and tell him that you have seen the crown jewels and feel that they look fake and that maybe he could do better, watch his face light up because he wouldn't have heard that for some years and will be intrigued as to who the hell you are and how do you know so much, once you open up the dialogue with Imee tell him what you have for sale and what you want, he will have you followed so be on your guard, initially stay overnight at a hotel and the following day go back to Imee and tell him to call off his lap dogs or you will release his story to the press."

"Strewth Charlie it sounds like something from a James Bond movie do you have to make it sound so melodramatic?" said Martin.
"No! "I could just leave you to it and see how fast you get arrested and charge with some little trumped up charge and lose your job and your life."
"Alright, alright I'm listening,"
Charlie went through everything, what price he should look at getting for nearly everything in the hidey hole and how much to pay Imee and what to do if I considered that Imee was taking too much. After it was over Charlie looked at the bewildered look on Martin's face and asked if he had any questions, there were millions of them but he couldn't think straight enough ask any particular one, so he said no and that he would take it all in and go and see Imee.

Chapter 4

Martin travelled to London by train all the time watching for anyone following him, just in case Imee had prior knowledge of him coming. The train seemed to be quite empty so it would be easy to spot anyone watching him.

He arrived at Euston Station and then caught a taxi to Bond Street and Imee's shop, it cost more but he didn't want to keep watching everyone, he was concerned about what he had brought with him for Imee to sell, he got out of the taxi and paid the driver and waited for it to pull away before he turned and pushed the intercom,

"Yes can I help you?"

"Yes I would like to see Imee Rosenberg the owner",

"One minute please"

Next a buzzing sound appeared and a voice telling him to push the door and walk up to the first floor, he did this and was greeted by a young receptionist,

"Please take a seat and Mr Rosenberg will be with you shortly",

That old joke of, 'don't call me shortly', came to his mind but he kept it to himself thankfully, strange he didn't feel a bit nervous even though he was about to make the biggest career move of his life, after this meeting there was no going back, he had spent a week working out his plan and now everything was coming to fruition and he was ok with it,

A rather large portly gentleman dressed in a pin stripped suit, sporting a full beard and wearing a skull cap on his head came out of the office and greeted him,

"How do you do, my name is Imee Rosenberg, do we have an appointment"?

"No sorry, my name is Martin McKay, and I just wanted to tell you that I saw the crown jewels the other day and they looked fake and maybe you could do better",

Imee nearly choked his eyes opened wider than Martin had seen anyone's do without popping out of there sockets,

"Sorry could you say that again", Martin repeated the quote that Charlie had told him,

"Thank you sir, would you like to come this way, Imee looked at his receptionist and told her to cancel all of his next two hour appointments and reschedule them for another day.

Once they entered the inner sanctum of his business Imee shut the door and then turned to Martin and said

"Who told you to say that and what do you want"?

"Charlie Rogers told me to look you up and ask you to do a couple of things for him",

"How do you know Charlie? he's in Prison"

"Yes and that's where I met him, we have been close friends for over twenty years now, but he is coming to the end of his time, he has cancer, but before he goes he asked me to come and see you for some help and assistance".

"What do you want?"

"I want you to set up a company for me, one that in effect has been established since 1965 and the company will be called 'The Maahes Trust and Savings Company', this company will purchase Insurance premiums that haven't matured yet, from people who were willing to receive early settlement figures, depending on the amount of time left on the premium would depend on the amount of monies they received, you will provide me with shares that I can give to whom ever I wished to and these people will receive a monthly income from these shares".

Imee listened intently making notes as Martin explained his requirements further, "This company will be legit, I want an accountant ensuring that all taxes are paid in full and a small number of employees".

Imee looked at him and then after a long pause said,"Is that all or do you require anything else?"

"No that's it, for the time being!"

"Good how do you expect to pay for all this, because if you think that just because you know a little about me that I'm going to pay, then I'm afraid you have another thing coming?"

"No, No, I want you to cash these in for me, Martin passed Imee three Bearer Bond all worth one hundred thousand dollars each, Imee's eyes lit up,

"You can have twenty percent and no more, is that agreed?" Imee looked at him and could see that there was going to be no haggling over the price so he agreed and they both shook hands, the deal was done,

Martin thanked him and told him that he would be back tomorrow to pick up the shares and the final details of the company etc.

Martin left the building and within minutes he spotted the tail, he walked to Canary Wharf and sat outside having a beer, he asked the waiter for the menu and as he looked into the window of the building in front of him he spotted the man again, this guy is rubbish at this, thought Martin and after finishing his meal he stayed there people watching wondering who they were and where were they going, he liked to people watch but he was still mindful of his shadow. He went to his hotel and booked in....

The receptionist at the hotel took all of his details and then in a sickly sweet voice announced that they had upgraded him to a suite,

"Thank you" he said signing the card she had given him,

"Room 421 Mr Smith and hope you enjoy your stay"

He walked over to the lift which was through a door with a glass panel in so he could still see the reception desk, he pressed the button and as he did so he looked over to reception desk, the man who had followed him was now speaking to young lady, he produced a leather wallet from his pocket and flashed his ID, immediately the lady started to find the card she had just written out, she handed it to him and made a note of the things that were on it, he turned to look in the direction of the lift and spotted me staring, he immediately handed her back the card and pretended to make polite conversation with her, she laughed and smiled, well more like grimaced, as the lift doors opened and he walked in.

Once in his room he placed everything away from his holdall and checked out the room, the room was massive, there was a living/kitchen/dining room with a large flat screen TV and then the bedroom which had another flat screen TV, a gigantic bed, writing bureau complete with mirror and a large wardrobe and finally a bathroom with bath, shower, toilet and sink the whole room was mirrored.

"If only the wife was here we could run around naked and none of the kids could disturb us, yeah right," he muttered to himself and she would be ringing them all night making sure everything was ok, that reminds me he thought I better give her a call and let her know that the meeting with sample testers is going fine. He was also thinking of completing the lie with telling her he'd just have to pop back in the morning to pick up some new leaflets that they have made up, she didn't need to know the real reason he was in London.

After making the call and sending his love to all of his children and his wife he made himself a cup of coffee and turned on the shower before going down to the bar for a night cap. The shower was one of those big powerful ones that nearly knocked you off your feet, it was like have a massage with water, he dried his body off then put his underwear on and sat in the lounge room and watched TV finishing his coffee, and thought "this is the life, not a care in the world," he watched the news whilst finishing getting dressed and went to the bar, the staff working in the hotel all seemed to be foreigners because they all had eastern European accents, "cheap labour", thought Martin.

The sounds of a football match were drifting from the TV so he watched it until the game finished and then went back to his room. As he entered the room he had an uncanny feeling that all was not well, he quickly went from one to another but no-one was there, he then checked the drawers and his holdall, someone had searched his belongings, were they after the bearer bonds and if so how did they know about them or was it something else? Imee he must have got his men to follow him and then search his room, Charlie was right, I would have to warn Imee about being too nosey.

In the morning he went down for breakfast early and as he walked into the restaurant area he spotted his shadow, he was already sat at a table eating his breakfast and trying to be nonchalant reading the morning paper. Martin got his breakfast and sat at his table, much to the shock of his shadow,

"Did you find what you were looking for last night"?

"Sorry do I know you"? said the MI5 man,

"You should do by now, you have been following me since I left Mr Rosenberg's establishment yesterday, by the way after breakfast I will be heading back there, just in case you get lost, if you want you can share a taxi with me, save all that pretending to look in shops, I'll wait outside."

Martin went to the Reception desk and paid his bill in cash and after picking up his receipt he walked to the Hotel entrance and waited for his taxi.

When the taxi arrived Martin got in and asked the driver to wait a minute, the MI5 man got in and they drove to Imee's, when they arrived the man got out but didn't go into the building, Martin paid the taxi driver and went inside to Imee offices. Imee had everything ready for him, the company had been registered and trading since 1965 and the accounts would stand up to and kind of scrutiny by either Her Majesties Government or any other agency that decided to take an interest in this business, the accountants were already being employed and the other staff would soon be employed.

"Why did you have me followed? Charlie told me to tell you if you know what's good for you stay out of what doesn't concern you, all you need to know is that we do business and that's it, your man is outside the building right now, because I've just given him a lift from my hotel, so what did your man find out for you after searching my gear?"

"You're a prison officer at HMP Patricroft and you have been there since leaving the RAF some years ago" said Imee,

"If you'd have asked me I would have told you all that, I'll be in touch if I need anything else, now call your pet dog off" said Martin.

"Listen I have a lot of powerful friends and since doing some work for them they tend to look out for me so when someone starts asking questions like you did I panicked and called in a favour that all, nothing sinister, I'm sorry you can never be too careful, I'll call him off, please take this",

Imee passed him his personal business card, with his contact details on it, "Use this number if you need to get in touch, or before you require another meeting ring me so that I can clear my schedule or arrange a different meeting place" Both men shook hands before parting company.

Chapter 5

All the way home on the train Martin read through all the paperwork Imee had given him, now that everything was ready he could start to involve all the others but he must be careful as to who he takes on, he made a mental list of who would be likely to accept his offer and be able to follow it through to the bitter end.

After a few days back at work he approached who he considered would be a good number two, Jamie Osborne he was aged fifty a heavy set and muscular six footer he was in the Army Intelligence and reached the rank of Sergeant, he joined at 17 and was posted throughout the world carrying out intelligence gathering for undercover operation for the military, during these operations he was away from home for long periods and during one of his stints away his eldest son got involved in drug taking; and due to being unable to pay off his debts he was beaten to within an inch of his life and ended up being brain dead for the rest of his days. This wasn't long as it happened because due to some complications his son died of a blood clot on his brain two and a half years later, no one was ever charged for the offence.

Jaymo decided to leave the Army so that he could be at home more with his wife, so after 12 years service to the Crown he joined the Prison Service, he was currently employed an officer in the Security Department, nickname Jaymo.

Jaymo and Martin had known each other for years, he met him and all the others he was going to invite to join him on this crusade at RAF Wroughton, this was where all servicemen and women were sent prior to being discharged from the service, this was to assist them with their reintegration back into civilian life, they also employed Medical Corp nurses and NHS Nurses to ensured all personnel were fit both physically and mentally, the Social workers were the families' liaisons officers to assist in the reintegration into civvy street for housing and such, finally the probation officers were used for counselling due to there expertise within this area and they also worked in the hospital as advisors.

Jaymo and the others during one of their bonding sessions had discussed the inadequate sentencing and the injustice of the legal system and how it had failed the victims, they all agreed that if they could they would like to even up the score against the criminals and ensure a more just sentence was imposed by either them or the judicial system, as it was just these eight in the room and on one else, some of the more out spoken members in the group let their feelings be known as to what they would do to re-adjust the balance of power, up to and including murder.

Martin asked Jaymo to meet him in Bury at the car park next to the old castle ruins at six o'clock, before going off duty Martin went to see old Charlie to find out how he was and if he had any more surprises for him, as he walked in, Charlie's pad mate walked out, "you've trained him well" he said,

"Knows where he stands with me"

"Nice to see you Martin, how'd it go in London, no problems with Imee"?

"No it all went well, you were right though he did have me followed, but we sorted that out straight away",

"I need to know Charlie is there any more things hiding in that place that I should know about or have you told me everything?"

"If you go into the room with the table in, go to the head of the table and there is a switch underneath, make sure nothing is on the table before flicking the switch, once the table turns it shows you the complete layout of the place, flick the switch again and it turns again hiding the model also if you haven't found it yet there is a light switch at the bottom of the stairs on the right.

That evening Martin met Jaymo in the car park and the two of them walked past the site and on to the local pub just next to the castle site, Jaymo found two seats in a corner and Martin brought the pints across,

"What's all the secrecy about?" asked Jaymo,

"Let me take you back some years now when we were at Wroughton and we were all sat in a room putting the Justice system to rights and getting fairness for the victims, remember?

"Yeah, we should even the score for the victims of those crimes the justice system had let down,"

"We'll what if I told you that we have the means and the know how and all we need now is to come up with a plan of action to carry out those plans. Would you believe me and not to put a finer point on it, would you still be interested in levelling the score for those who were unjustly treated by the courts?"

"You mean killing cons?" said Jaymo,

Martin nodded,

"Oh Christ Martin, who else have you discussed this idea with",

"No-one just you, you're my first recruit and hopefully my right hand man",

Jaymo sat quietly taking in what he had been asked to do and then finally he turned to Martin and said,

"I'm in, but we must be careful who we recruit and where we hold our meetings to decide who will be our victims",

"Don't worry about holding meetings; I have something to show you",

The two men finished their pints and then walked to Martin's car; he opened the doors and took out a flash light, then turned and told Jaymo to follow him and watch.

Martin walked off towards the castle ruins closely followed by Jaymo, they headed towards the hidden entrance and Martin showed Jaymo the eye and how it opened the door way, Jaymo gasped but never spoke, he followed and Martin ushered him inside and closed the door behind them.

Turning his flash light on, the two of them looked at each other and laughed, Martin went on ahead leading them further down the stairs towards the centre, when at last it opened up that's when Jaymo grabbed Martin's arm and said,

"How the hell did you know about this place?"

"Just wait and I'll tell you everything, but first let me show you around",

Martin put his hand on the wall to the right of him searching in the dark for the light switch, when he found it he turned it on and lit the place up; Jaymo looked on in amazement he was like a kid in a toy shop.

They walked into the room with the massive round table in and Martin walked over to the end of the table, felt underneath and found the switch",

"Just mind yourself, step back",

As Jaymo did so the table turned over showing a scale model of the underground hidey hole, even Martin was impressed by the shear scale of the model and realised that he had only touched on the place during his first visit.

"Take a seat and I'll tell you everything, but this must go no further until we decide who else to involve",

Martin told him the whole story about Charlie and Imee, his trip to London and the MI5 man, Jaymo listened without interrupting and when finally Martin had finished, he looked at him and said,

"Well that's everything that you need to know, there are something's that I have left out but those are for your safety so you can deny any previous knowledge",

Now about this place there is only one rule no-one but no-one goes in the safe room, that is out of bounds for you and

everyone else who comes down here, and ask no questions and you will be told no lies about that room, agreed?"
Jaymo nodded and then the two of them looked at the model in front of them and Martin explained the escape routes and how they worked.

Chapter 6

He would leave Jaymo down there to get used to the place and also to clean it up while he went off to gather the rest of the Brotherhood, Both he and Jaymo had discussed who they had in mind and both were in agreement about those that had been chosen.

Martin's number two was now confirmed; Alan Jones aged fifty four he was plump but built hard, five foot nine, he had previously completed two thirds of his medical training at Edinburgh University before having to leave due to his parents being killed in a car accident; the driver of the vehicle was intoxicated and high on drugs.

AJ came home and after the funeral decided to join the Army as a medic, after passing his initial training with honours he was posted to his first station in Hereford, during a training exercise he was requested by the commander of the SAS to join his regiment as a combat medic, he was with Daz at the Embassy siege but their paths never crossed until they met at RAF Wroughton with the others, he had followed Daz and his crew all around the world, he never finished his full medical training but during his time with the SAS whilst in Borneo and Asia he became interested in poisons and venomous spiders and vertebrate and their effects on humans, he became somewhat of an expert on the subject and created many new antidotes for some of the more venomous snakes and also had books published which are still being used by the Armed Forces today.

He decided to become a civilian and to lay some roots of his own so he moved back to the house his parents had left him and joined the prison service as a medical officer he had befriended a few of the officers at RAF Wroughton prior to leaving the armed forces and met them again at HMP Patricroft, now employed as a Healthcare officer, nickname AJ.

Third in line was Alan Palmer he was fifty two plump but muscular, he had arms like Popeye, his wife gave him the name Albear due to his family coming from Canada and setting up home in England when he was ten, he still had a bit of a twang of the French Canadian but only his wife seemed to notice it. He had joined Royal Air Force and was a linguist based at Liege in Belgium at the N.A.T.O. Headquarters there to assist the top brass with any language barriers that they had, during his time there he had a run in with one of the top brass and decided that he would sit him on his backside for the way in which he spoke to the future Mrs Palmer and with one punch he did, at his Court Marshall all of the charges were dropped due to the fact that

Alan had hired a barrister from England who just tied the young officers who were pretending to be barristers in knots, he was however transferred to another station and Mrs Palmer followed him shortly after their wedding.

In the Christmas of the same year Albear's grandmother was attacked and robbed in her own home, she died just over twelve months later due to complications with her operation on her hip, the offender got two months.

Albear joined the prison service after becoming disheartened by the way in which he was treated after the incident with the high ranking officer and the fact that he wasn't there for his grandmother, on joining the prison service he was posted to HMP Patricroft and was employed as an Allocations officer, nickname Albear.

They both decided on Daryl Green this man was 49 years old a muscular and athletic looking individual, approximately five foot nine, a good looking guy for his age, but always quiet and unassuming, he was always watching and taking everything on board before he would move, never lost his temper and always spoke softly and quietly, these were the qualities that Jaymo liked best and Martin had to agree with him.

Daryl joined the Army at sixteen and a half and moved up the ranks to L/Corporal and then applied to join the SAS he was the youngest person to pass the gruelling selection process and at 18 he was sent to Borneo to complete his Jungle training, on his return he was stationed in London carrying out close protection duties, during this time he started dating a young secretary who worked in the Iranian embassy, he became engaged to be married in July 1980 unfortunately on the 5th of May 1980 six gunmen took over the Iranian embassy in Kensington and during this siege his future wife was killed by the gunmen, Daz was part of the team who stormed the embassy to rescue the hostages in Operation Nimrod, five Iranian gunmen were killed and one was arrested and given a life sentence.

After that he volunteered only for operations in hostile territories and assisted in numerous dangerous undercover operations for his country, after having a physiological assessment done on him after one of these operations he was discharged from the forces on medical grounds, currently employed at HMP Patricroft as a wing officer, nickname Daz.

And last but not least they recruited David Hillard he was fifty four a wiry looking guy but as fit as a butchers dog still at his age, David had been in the Navy as a civil engineer, he joined the Marines after completing all of his training and had been in the Falklands during the war and had also been part of a team sent on a fact finding mission to Argentina during this conflict, unbeknown to the Argentinean and the British Governments this was purely military operation.

The team had been dropped off at night and told to find their own way back, they did when they stole a Bell 222 helicopter from the Argentinean airfield, only to be shot at by their own forces when they attempted to return back to base, they all survived and the aircraft was kept as a trophy.

After this tour of duty he returned home and this is when his troubles started he had developed both a drink and gambling problem either of which was bad enough but both together was too much, on numerous occasions he would end up in the Accident and Emergency Unit of the local Hospital after being beaten up and all of his possessions being stolen off him.

The man showed great strength of character by overcoming both of these problems but the strain on his marriage was too much and his wife left him taking the children with her, he was also at this time retired from the Navy on medical and personal grounds, he was a wing officer at HMP Patricroft but had no nickname stating that he was too old for that rubbish.

The first recruit he would contact would be A.J. he was a medic and would come in useful if any medical issues came into play such as overdose etc, after him Martin would carry on until he had all of them on there list, he picked up the telephone and started dialled everyone on his list to arrange a meeting that would be far enough away so as not to draw attention to themselves but also in case any of them turned him down.

As they arrived at the Conference centre they were escorted to a large room there was tea, coffee and biscuits they were told to help themselves, as the others started to arrive and were shown to the room they began to recognise each other and then started to question as to why they had been asked to come here, none of them had the slightest idea.

One of the ushers come back to the room and asked each one in turn to follow them to a separate room where they met Martin and Jaymo.

Martin opened up with the formalities by talking about how was the journey, any problems finding the place and the weather and such things, whilst all the time Jaymo was observing their body language, they went into how's the family, work etc and the questions kept going until both Jaymo and Martin were satisfied that they had made the right choice and that they felt that now was the time to ask them the question and inform them as to the real reason they had been chosen, to join the crusade and the brotherhood. After they were told Martin and Jaymo sat back and watched as the reality and the severity of what they had been asked suddenly hit home, As the interviews went on the easier it got in spotting the right choices, they informed them that they were under no obligation and could leave at any time but to assist them both Martin and Jaymo reminded them of what they had said in their sessions at RAF Wroughton and how they had lost family members and that the perpetrators had got away with such pitiful sentences, some of them agreed straight away to be recruited into the brotherhood, others asked if they could sleep on it and get back to them the following day, this was agreed and Jaymo stated that he would expect a call from them by dinner time, they were asked not to discuss anything with the others just in case.....

By the following day all of the recruits had contacted Jaymo and agreed to become part of the brotherhood, they were all told to meet Jaymo in the car park next to the ruins in Bury, once they were all there they were shown how to access the hide out by Jaymo who would show them around the meeting place and set them some work to carry out so as to make the place cleaner and less of an assault course, after showing them the model of the place they were all sent off to check out the tunnels.

After they had had a good look around and familiarised themselves with their surroundings and which exit took you where, they all returned to the now renamed boardroom and took a seat.

Martin then knocked on the table to gain their attentions and said,

"Gentlemen welcome to the Brotherhood of the Maahes, our quest will be to right the wrongs that have been committed by the courts and as such we will endeavour to carry out these rights without harming any innocents, do you all agree to up hold this quest",

As in one voice they came back with "Yes".

He took all the relevant personal details off each of them i.e. bank account numbers addresses wife's name etc and would pass these on to the accountants running the business, he then issued each one with there share certificate and explained that they were to keep these in a safe place and if anyone asked about them they were to tell them that they purchased them with their discharge grants from the forces.

They were informed that each month they would receive a nominal amount of money, but they were not to sell these shares to anyone, if they had any financial or personnel problems they were to tell either him or Jaymo straight away, where the money came from was not any of there concerns and the least they knew the better it would be if it went pear shaped, they were to tell no-one about each other, about the brotherhood, about this place or bring anyone here, if your wife's started to get worried as to where you keep going tell her that you joined the masons that should satisfy her curiosity if not then make something else up.

"Once we begin this quest there will be no turning back until it has been completed, are there any questions?", the room remained silent, Martin looked around the room but no-one said anything, "Ok then gentlemen just for a warm up, Jaymo has scoured the files of some potential clients for us to peruse over and decide our first candidate", Jaymo passed out files to each of them and they all started to open them up and decide, after about an hour or so David spoke first,

"I vote for this one", he held up the file of a prisoner called Michael Lowe, currently serving 5 years for rape, according to this information though the woman killed her self after the court case because she couldn't live with the thought of him coming out in two and a bit years and her worry was that she might bump into him in the street when she was out shopping and also the shame she felt that she had brought on her family by not fighting back more, She left two children aged 7 and 11 and a husband".

They all agreed with the choice and set aside the other files which Jaymo collected and put away for another day,

"Ok gents now we have to decide who we need to plan how, where and when and also we need to know which of us will be the first to carry out this task", said Martin.

Everyone looked at each other then out of the blue David said,

"As I was the one who put this particular gentleman forward I feel that it's only right that I get first crack of the whip, now I will need some assistance and it will require some planning",

Everybody got their diaries out so that they could coordinate when they would be available to assist, A.J. told them that next week he would be on duty all week to help if need be and this was quickly followed by Albear they decided on a week that they would all be in, it just so happened that Martin and Jaymo were in that week as well, they got together and between them they decided on a day that suited all of them, how they would do it and where they would commit the task, it wasn't a crime to them it was justice and they justified it to themselves as they were only doing what the courts should have done in the first place.

On the day in question, a stand fast roll check was called, this was a perfect cover for them as everyone would be busy on there own wings and hopefully wouldn't notice David and Albear, for the first operation everything went according to plan, the two of them slipped in, carried out the deed and then David went off first watched by Albear and then after the staff had initially attended the scene and as they busied themselves with saving the prisoners life and calling for assistance he slipped back to the fours on H Wing, that night they all met at the secret hide out and went through the whole operation making sure every angle had been planned for and dealt with, they got reports of the incident from Jaymo and A.J. the medic, Jaymo stated that the Police had been contacted and the cell sealed off, they asked if he had left a note and they were told no,

"Doesn't matter we'll write it down as another suicide, we will be in tomorrow to pick up the paperwork,"

A.J. informed them that the Doctor had completed the death certificate and had put down suicide as the course of death,

"So it seems that our first task was a complete success, well done gentlemen, we will adjourn to the local tavern for a liquid libation or for you more common people, lets go for a pint in the pub", said Martin

They all laughed as they stood up to go and as like well trained soldiers the first four who came out chose different exits, Martin looked at Jaymo and smiled as he said, "What a great team, they automatically went different routes without being asked, see you in the pub the beers are on me,"

They all cheered as they went down the tunnels, about fifteen minutes later they were all in the pub knocking back bitter and lager shandy's because they were all driving, after they had supped up Martin told them to meet again in a weeks time same place at six o'clock any problems they were to inform Jaymo straight away and we will sort it out.

After all the rest had left Martin and Jaymo remained and went over how they would carry out the next one without drawing suspicion to the Prison and especially to themselves, Jaymo mentioned that the DST (Dedicated search team) had found what they thought was pure heroin, he would adopt a quantity of the substance and replace it with talcum powder so as not to draw any suspicion on the DST or himself he would also get a small syringe from the Healthcare with A.J.'s assistance, if they were to give this to

a prisoner who used to take drugs as some of the one's on their list had, it would kill them for sure, giving them
a massive overdose would stop their heart in it's tracks, the two of them agreed and Jaymo would relieve the DST of a quantity of pure heroin.

At the brotherhoods next meeting Martin informed them of how the next prisoner was to die and that the one's they could choose from had to be current or ex junkies, Jaymo passed out the files that fitted the criteria and they would now have to decide which one, who would carry out this execution and when.

Daz was the first to speak, he held up a file with the name McBain on,

"This piece of shit gets my vote, he killed an eighty six year old ex-soldier because he wanted money for drugs he tortured the old man into revealing where his money was and after getting the money he smashed his skull in with a picture of the old man and his wife, and then ransacked the house.

He was given two years for manslaughter because he claimed diminished responsibility due to drugs and alcohol and the Judge believed him",.

Daz said that he wanted to do this one, Martin and Jaymo would assist him, on the day in question all three met on the centre and went onto D wing, the wing was quiet because the staff were out doing shop moves and the prisoners were busy going to work or education, Daz went into Mac's cell and hid a syringe full of heroin under the mattress on his bunk, Mac had told the staff that he would harm any other prisoner if he had to share so they made him single cell occupancy so he didn't have to share with anyone, this helped their cause.

Daz came out of the cell and all three walked off, "It's in the cell under the top bunk mattress; all we need to do now is tell Mac where he can find his present,"

Jaymo stated that he was on overtime tonight and he would ensure that he got placed on "D" wing by tell the Principal Officer on the centre that he was checking out a snitch, it all went according to plan and when Jaymo was helping the wing staff bang up at lock up he made sure that he was the one checking that all the cell doors were locked and secure, as he got to Mac's door and passed a note under it, the note told Mac where to find his present, Jaymo watched at the spy hole as Mac found the syringe, he was like a kid at a sweetie shop, tying off his upper arm his veins protrude out, this was because he hadn't shot up in a long time so his veins came to the surface quickly, he dug the needle into his arm and pushed the plunger all the way taking in every last drop, he then drew out some blood and then pushed the plunger again, this made sure that all of the heroin was taken in, after that he then lay on his bed to await the sudden rush, Jaymo walked away slowly so as not to draw any unwanted attention to himself, when he arrived at the wing office he signed as checking the doors and left, he met Martin and Daz in the car park,

"It's done, he won't see tomorrow,"

They all walked off to their cars and drove off all feeling proud of themselves another job well done, thought Martin.

That night Martin slept soundly knowing that another piece of human excrement was off the street for good.

Chapter 7

Early in the morning about 02:00hours the house phone rang, Martin picked it up and answered, it was Jaymo,
"Sorry to disturb you this early but could you meet me in the Prison car park about 06:00 this morning as I have some information for you; Martin agreed to be there and would bring the coffee,
"Not so much sugar this time you always put too much in,"
"I have a sweet tooth, but I'll put a little less in, see you in a few hours",

At 06:00 hours Martin was sat in his car on the Prison car park waiting, he poured himself a coffee and as he lifted his head up after putting his flask in the cup holder on the console he saw Jaymo's car come into the car park, Jaymo parked near to him and then got out and walked over and got in Martin's motor, he was handed a cup of coffee,
"Go on then what's that matter", said Martin
"They discovered Mac's body early this morning and phoned me at home; they want a team together this morning to spin the whole wing for drugs as they believe that someone on there has supplied Mac with pure heroin,"

"Jaymo take it easy no-one knows about us, if this had happened without our interference would they have done what they are asking you to do now,"

"Yes, "said Jaymo,

"Right so they don't know about us, just do your job as you would have done anyway, who have you rang to come in with you, any of our lot,

Martin looked at Jaymo as he went through the list he rang last night,

"Ah AJ, I rang him because we need a medic in case anyone else has taken this drug",

"Good we will wait for AJ and bring him up to speed, then the two of you can look after each other, if you need any more help, just tell who ever is in charge that you have seen me in the car park and that I may have gone to G wing and he should ring me to assist you lot, ok",

"Jaymo agreed just as AJ appeared at the driver's door, Martin wound the window down,

"What you two up to?" said AJ,

Martin explained the situation and what they were to do AJ nodded and the two of them walked in together followed shortly afterwards by Martin.

Jaymo took his team onto the wing and assigned them into teams of three and set them off on each landing to start spinning the cells looking for and contraband, as they passed Mac's cell AJ noticed that it had been sealed by the night staff and was awaiting the Police and the Coroners Officer to investigate.

Jaymo went to the centre office and spoke to the Principal Officer and the night Senior Officer regarding the incident, "morning gents" said Jaymo "who found the body and when?"

The PO pointed to the young officer sat in the corner drinking sweet tea and shaking; the Officer looked at Jaymo and said,

"Whilst on my rounds I went to Mac's cell and knocked on the door, he didn't move even when I shouted him, he just lay there so I called the centre office that's when the P.O. and S.O. came onto the wing and we all went in, I shook him but nothing, so I pulled the cover off his face and that's when I realised he was dead, as I moved in closer I kicked the needle under the bed, but I didn't pick it up I just left it there, it's still under the bed",

Jaymo looked at the P.O.,

"I called for medical assistance over the radio net "said the P.O.

The Medical Officer arrived on the wing about five minutes later and checked Mac's vitals and stated that in his opinion he was dead, but they would still need to call an ambulance as per the protocol for death in custody, we called Comms on the phone and requested a blue light, this arrived fifteen minutes later and was escorted to the wing, the paramedic stated that Mac was indeed dead and requested a Doctor to come into the prison and confirm, the Duty Doctor was called and he pronounced him dead at 01.45 hours this morning. After informing the Duty Governor of the death in custody he told me to ring you and get you to put a team together, get you in here this morning first thing and that where we are up to."

Jaymo thought too himself well if that's all that's happened there is no need for me to be so paranoid about this, he thanked God and then went into automatic mode and carried on with his mini investigation he took the key to the lock barring entry to the cell and went and checked the cell, he would give it a quick sweep to see if there was a note, he entered the cell and on the table he noticed his note to Mac, he picked it up and put it in his pocket the P.O. with him failed to notice anything untoward so Jaymo then resealed the cell and said that he would write his report for the Governor in which he would state that the prisoner had taken his own life by accident due to drug overdose and that the night staff had followed the correct protocol throughout the incident, the P.O. thanked him and they both left.

Jaymo went to his office and wrote his report for the number one Governor, as he'd want it later that morning, he rang Martin and told him everything was fine and they had nothing to worry about, he had retrieved the note and was in the process of destroying it as they spoke he then hung up. After getting rid of the note he rang the Police Liaison Officer and informed him what had occurred and in Jaymo's opinion he thought that Mac had taken his own life by injecting himself and having a massive overdose of heroin causing his heart to stop, Jaymo had seen quite a few of these and the PLO knew this and took Jaymo at his word and stated that he would contact the Coroners Officer and the Investigating Officer and tell them to contact Jaymo at there earliest convenience for an up to date report so that this matter could be expedited to allow the prison to continue to use the cell.

Jaymo thanked him and hung up, he then rang Martin and told him,

"Feel better now?"

Jaymo said he did and put the phone down.

The Coroners Officer came in and Jaymo took him to the cell, unsealed the door so as to allow him to take photographs and pick up the evidence and make out his report a copy of which he gave to Jaymo, he was then returned to the gate and allowed to leave.

Jaymo attended the morning meeting and explained as to his finding about the suicide and the results that his team had come up with,

"The Coroners Officer is happy that this is a suicide and has given me the report which state such, my teams have found a small quantity of cannabis, hooch, a home made tattooing gun and numerous bits of burnt foil, but no heroin on the wing, it's either all gone or it was acquired elsewhere.

"Thank you Jaymo you can leave now", said the Governor,

Jaymo turn around and walked out of the office, still listening to the Governor speaking to his underlings about this being the second suicide in a couple of months and wanting to know what the hell was going on in his Prison.

Chapter 8

At 12.30 hours Friday November the 13th 1992 the call went out on the radio net for the Hospital Officer to attend G wing urgently, Martin was sat in the mess with Jaymo having there dinner, they both looked at each other,

"It's nothing to do with us is it?" said Martin,

"No, but I'll go to channel two and see if I can get any more information," Jaymo changed channel and then put his hand up to his ear piece, he then looked at Martin and said,

"Best you get back to your Wing; it's old Charlie's seems he's in a bad way,"

Martin told Jaymo he would see him later and then got up and left his dinner half eaten, he walked quickly cursing every closed and locked gate, walking up the main drag of the prison he acknowledge all the staff leaving for either dinner or finishing their shifts.

When he reached the wing he went straight to the office, some of the wing staff were there and one of the young officers informed him that they thought that old Charlie had kicked the bucket or if not he was close to,

"Be a bit more respectful will you, you are supposed to be professional", the S.O. snapped,

"Sorry, but he is only an old con,"

If looks could kill then this guy should have dropped dead where he stood, one of the more senior members of staff dragged the young officer away before Martin did something they would all regret later. The young officer looked at the others as if to say what have I done wrong, he was informed as to why this particular prisoner was different to the rest of them.

When the two officers returned the youngster apologised for his stupidity, Martin nodded and then walked down to the one's landing, A.J. came out of the cell as Martin approached he walked over to him and took hold of his arm,
"Old Charlie's in a bad way, he is going to go to outside hospital but there is no hope for him, the Doctors coming across but I doubt if he will come up with anything different than I have told you".
Martin walked down to Charlie's cell, the officers left as did the other Medical Officer, when it was just the two of them, Charlie looked up at Martin and said,
"Don't be sad mate I've had a good life even when I got caught and sent down I'm still glad because I met you and even though we have had our differences we still remained friends, thank you Martin",

"No Charlie thank you, if every con was like you my job would be so much easier,"

"The one thing I do regret" said Charlie ,

"Is that we never got to meet outside these walls, so I could take you for a drink and although I know your family from afar I wish I'd have met them",

"Charlie before it's too late I need to tell you something," Martin replied,

"About the money and the other things that you gave me, I need to tell you what it will be used for,"

"I don't need to know, it's yours to do with as you wish,"

There was a pregnant pause before Martin continued,

"Charlie we are using it to rectify what we consider to be the injustices that the courts hand out to murderers, rapists and the like by giving out real sentences like the death penalty".

Martin hadn't noticed that old Charlie had passed away quietly just listening to him, he hadn't even made a noise, Martin looked at him and shouted for AJ, Charlie just lay there with his eyes wide open but there was no life in them

AJ ran in to the cell,

"What's up?"

Martin pointed to Charlie but didn't say anything,

AJ took his pulse, looked at Martin and shook his head,

"He's gone, sorry mate,"

Martin walked out of the cell; he looked like he had the troubles of the world on his shoulders, with his head down he walked up the landing and went upstairs to his office as he went in he slammed the door behind him, he picked up the phone at the same time he took his wallet out of his pocket and removed the business card and giving a big sigh he dialled the number.

Imee picked up the ringing phone,

"Sorry to be the bearer of bad news Imee but Charlie has just passed away, would you please ring this number and inform them that you will be dealing with the funeral arrangements", said Martin giving Imee the Prison number, Imee passed on his condolences and told him he would ring back with the details as soon as he could, and then hung up. That night Martin rang Imee again and asked him to give him the relevant information about the funeral arrangements, Jaymo called for Martin at his home and the two of them went out to the local pub and had a toast to an old friend.

The funeral took place on the following Friday at a small church in Agecroft, it was drizzling with rain as though the earth had shed a tear for old Charlie. Martin drove into the Cemetery and parked in the public car park next to the main gate, he got out of his car and walked slowly towards the small church in the grounds, Charlie would have liked this place it was quiet, there were lots of trees and the breeze was blowing leaves up into the church area.

Next to the cemetery was the canal and you could hear the water lapping against the side walls as a small boats had just gone past, it was peaceful, he stood in the doorway and awaited the arrival of the hearse with old Charlie's remains inside, he didn't have to wait long the hearse came first followed by a black limousine as the hearse pulled up the bearers got out and went to the back of the vehicle, Martin moved so he could catch a glimpse of who was in the limo he had an idea but wanted to be sure, it was who he thought, it was Imee, Martin walked up to him and shock his hand,

"Is this it just you and me," said Imee,

"Afraid so, he didn't make many friends inside that would be allowed out unescorted and he didn't have any family that we knew of",

They both walked in behind the coffin and took a seat at the front, the local vicar came out and thanked them for turning up, just then there was a noise at the rear of the church both Imee and Martin turned around, it was the rest of the brotherhood, they had all taken the day off work to see off an old friend and to support their leader, Jaymo walked up to Martin and shock his hand,

"Didn't think we would let him go without saying goodbye did you, besides we figured you'd need some support as well",

Martin looked around and mouthed the words "Thank you," the vicar cleared his throat and the service began.

It was a good service and Imee had done Charlie proud and Martin told Imee so, they shook hands and then just before they parted company Martin handed him some more bearer bonds to put into the company business, Imee took them and then told him he would be in touch,

"By the way this is for you", said Imee,

Imee passed Martin an A4 size envelope, which he opened, inside were the proof of purchases for the art work and the authenticity letters from Sotheby's.

"Congratulations you're now one of the richest men in England", said Imee,

"Thank you Imee, and thank you Charlie," said Martin,

"If there is anything you need call me, as it stands you are my new best friend and hopefully I can have a profitable relationship as I had with Charlie", the two shook hands.

Imee got into the waiting limo and the driver shut the door, walked around to the drivers door got in and drove away, leaving Martin stood there holding the letter, The brotherhood gathered around him and Jaymo said,

"Let's go and have a pint on old Charlie,"

Martin said he would buy the drinks, as they walked towards the car park Jaymo asked Martin about the envelope and the gentleman in the limo,

"No need to concern yourself about either of those things Jaymo, all you need to know is that our quest will be continuing for sometime to come thanks to a benefactor from heaven".

Chapter 9

A few days later Martin asked the brotherhood to meet at the hideout at seventeen hundred hours, so that he could explain about the two previous sentences that they had delivered and about the Governors troubles.
All of them except Martin arrived on time, Jaymo looked around,
"Has anyone seen Martin or do they know if he has been held up for any reason?"
"Daz stated that he had seen him early that day and had said that he would see me tonight,"
Just as they were about to start the meeting Martin flung the door open all in the room jumped and then seeing who it was shouted out obscenities at him,
Holding his hand up to stop them and trying too catch his breath, he eventually spoke,
"I'm being followed I think that I gave them the slip, but from work all the way home and to this place, I managed to get ahead of them and give myself some time to get in here without being seen, but I think they are in the car park next door, all of them rose to there feet but Martin put his hand up and motioned them to sit back down,

"Jaymo, Daz come with me, he could see the files had been handed out so he said, the rest of you take a look at the files on the desk and consider our next client for punishment,"

All three walked out of the room and Martin closed the door behind them,

"Jaymo you go to the exit near the church, Daz you go to the cemetery and I'll go to the one near the Library we will meet in the local pub next to the car park keep your eyes open,"

They all went off in different directions, Martin was the last to make it to the pub, Jaymo and Daz had joined up just next to the church and had scouted

the area for anyone who looked suspicious who were being particular about the cars or the ruins, it didn't take long to notice them, two well dressed individuals, Daz spotted them first and then he made Jaymo aware of them,

"MI5", said Daz,

"How do you know",

"Trust me I know,"

"Get to the pub; we can still keep an eye on them without making it so obvious",

Daz got the seats near the window which over looked the ruins and the car park and Jaymo got all of them a drink, as he walked to the table with the drinks Martin entered, Daz gestured him over and then pointed out the two gentlemen,

"Crap MI5, how the hell have then got onto us so quickly, or is it something else?"

"How would you like to know where they go?" said Jaymo,

"Sorry",

Martin went to the public telephone in the pub and dialled Imee on his personal number, Imee answered straight away,

"Hello,

"Imee its Martin,

"Hello how can I be of assistance to you",

"I am being followed by two MI5 officers, do you know why and who has put them up to it?"

Martin was under the impression Imee would know because it was him, checking on his new business friend,

"Listen it's not me but I will check with my contacts, can you ring me back in an hour on this number?"

"Martin agreed and hung up",

He went back to the table and watched as these two guys checked out all of the vehicles on the car park,

"We need to know why they are following me and who has put them up to it",

Jaymo smiled at them,

"What's up with you have you just dropped your guts, you dirty"…….

"No I haven't but I do have a nice little surprise for our unwanted guests",

"What?" the other two said.

Jaymo pulled a small GPS tracker out of his pocket, and asked the two of them to keep the two gents busy while he planted it on there vehicle and off he went, Daz and Martin headed outside to confront these two but as they came out of the pub the two MI5 men spotted Martin and started to come towards them,

"Lets take these two for a wonder around Bury see if they like it", said Daz,

So the two set off at a cracking pace, the two MI5 men found it difficult to keep up with them and when they had taken them far enough away from the car park they lost them.

Martin and Daz made it back to the hide out, when they got back inside the safe heaven Jaymo was in there and looking at the GPS screen with the others,

"Is it working?" said Daz",

"Come and have a look, we will know every move those two buggers will be doing, unless they find the tracker"

After about ten minutes a shout went out there on the move, they all gathered around to watch were they went to,

"According to the GPS they are at a Masonic lodge just outside of Bolton near Little Lever, why would they go there and why are they following us?"

"Ok gentlemen sit down lets get back to business, we can figure what they were after later, we need to choose our next client," said Martin"

"It's alright, said AJ, we have done it while you lot were out gallivanting about town we decided on this one." Holding up the file on Harry Morse, "he is a paedophile who has over the last twenty years preyed on little girls, he has rape, tortured, molested and killed forty children, but never served more than six years because he states that he has a mental condition and it was backed up by some Doctors that his defence Barrister has found, his girlfriend would seem to be involved but they struck a deal with the Prosecution and she was never charged, her name is Lauren Walker she was supposed to have brought the children to Morse so he could carry out his vile acts on them, the Judge had to advise the jury that Morse could not be held responsible for his actions if he is found to be mentally impaired."

"Why don't we make the Doctors and Barrister our clients?" said Daz",

"No we are not going there," said Martin and Jaymo in unison, "They were only doing their jobs, this brotherhood was set up to right the wrongs the courts have done not the people who work in them they will have to sleep with the decisions that they made,"

"Right are we all in agreement about this client",

They all shout yes as one,

"Now how are we going to do it and when and by whom", said Jaymo,

AJ stood up, "I will assist you with this one as I have some medical information that will help to eliminate the client, without putting any suspicion on us",

"Do tell", said Martin,

"Last month we carried out some allergy tests not on Morse but his cell mate, when I've gone to check the results, I noticed a rash on Morse's arm, he is highly allergic to nuts",

"How the hell is that going to kill him", said Alan,

"If he is exposed to enough nuts it will cause him to go into an anaphylactic shock and without an adrenaline injection he will die",

"Good one", said Alan, I'll help you, how are we going to do it though",

"How about we find out when he is next on a domestic visit and look at exposing him to nuts in the main visits hall, by the time anyone realises what's happened and they call for emergency assistance he should be well out of it, hopefully", said David,

AJ agreed to bring some nut oil into the prison in a highly concentrated mix, he would then pass it on to Martin, he would then find out when Morse was on a visit and before anyone else was in that day he would go up to the visits hall and he would spray all of the vulnerable prisoners tables with the nut oil, this should ensure wherever Morse sat he would come into contact with the oil.

When they had agreed who it should be Martin told them to talk amongst themselves for a bit while he found out if his contact had found out why he was being followed, he went to the telephone box and rang Imee,

"Did you manage to find out who and why I'm being followed", said Martin,

"Yes, MI5 are concerned about the transactions of the company you set up the think it may be a terrorist organisation that have set up a dummy corporation",

"Hang on you told me that the company was legit and would stand any type of scrutiny from any Government agency, now what are you saying",

"Its fine I have spoken to my contact and he assures me that your company is sound and the two guys are about to be called back to London, that is after they have checked out some other suspicious activity in the Manchester area, so don't worry your safe".

We need to have a meeting regarding what is going to happen with the stuff that old Charlie has left me, I can't leave it where it is, I want to sell one of the paintings and give some of the proceeds to certain charities I think Charlie would have approved of, give me a month and will you come to Manchester and see me, you can stay at the Midlands Hotel and add it to the costs that we decide that your share will be, Ok?"

Imee agreed and the two of them hung up.

Martin went back to the hide out and told the others, but he still reminded all of them to be careful when driving anywhere and make sure that you're not being followed, if there are any concerns then take the car registration and tell either myself or Jaymo as soon as possible.

Chapter 10

"Right gentlemen good night and good hunting, remember not to leave from the same exit and ensure that the coast is clear before exiting, take care",

Friday afternoon the visits list came out for Saturday, Sunday and Monday and sure as eggs where eggs there was Morse's name. Monday morning 09.45 Morse being visited by his girlfriend Lauren Walker, everything was go for Monday, Martin came in early as usual and went to his office, put on a pair of latex gloves and took the oil spray in it's clean sealed box and then set off for main visits, when he reached the hall he first made sure the coast was clear, it was, the staff wouldn't be in for another thirty minutes, he took the bottle out of his pocket he opened the box and began to spray every vulnerable prisoner table in the main hall, he even sprayed the chairs at the tables, when he was done he checked the bottle and he only had a small quantity left, he smiled to himself and as he was leaving he went through the holding room area and opened the vulnerable prisoners holding room door and sprayed the seats in there, just to make sure and then he left.

AJ had been told by Martin that he should ring in that day to say he wouldn't be coming in as he had a domestic emergency his Senior Officer told him if he need anything to give him a call,
"NO, I'll be fine and I'll see you tomorrow, it should be sorted today, thanks anyway",

Around about ten o'clock a call went out over the radio for urgent medical assistance required in the main visits hall, Hotel 1 the duty medical officer responded, she made it to the visits hall and was shown to Morse's table where he had collapsed on the floor clutching his throat, the nurse bent down and asked his visitor what he had taken, she said nothing so the nurse looked directly at her the visitor was in her late forties about six foot, eighteen stone with large breast, "good god the size of her what ever day she says it is!, it is" thought the nurse, she quickly repeated the question, that was when she noticed that the women was now struggling to breath and was holding her throat, then it happened the women just clutched her chest and fell forward as straight as a die right onto her face. The sound of her face hitting the floor was horrendous, it was like someone hitting a water melon with a cricket bat, her head just burst, the blood sprayed out splattering everyone close by, the nurse got to her and check for a pulse, there was nothing, by the time she had hit the floor she was dead, the nurse looked at the other staff and shouted for them to get a blue light for her ASAP.

Morse grabbed her arm and squeezed hard and then went limp, she checked his vitals but it was of little use she knew he was dead, the Duty Doctor and the Duty Governor along with the Security S.O. turned up, the Doctor informed the Governor that he suspected some kind of adverse reaction to something that they had eaten but he wasn't sure, they would have to wait for the autopsy, all the visitors were filed out of the main visits room and the prisoners were returned to there wings, the Coroners Officer turned up and they removed the body.

At about twelve o'clock to two visits cleaning ladies turned up and then started to clean the visits area wiping down all of the furniture and unbeknown to them removing all of the evidence, by the time they had finished there was not a hint of any nut oil and they then started to Hoover the floor when they got about half way through the Security S.O., Police Liaison Officer, Detective Sergeant and a Scenes of crime Officer turned up, when they saw these two cleaners the Security S.O. screamed for them to stop cleaning, they both turned around and shouted back at the group that they were not to mess up[the place as they had just finished cleaning, the Security S.O. asked them where they had started and when they showed him and all the others with him, they then asked if they could be returned to the gate as the scene had been compromised and all the evidence if there had been any would have been contaminated or removed and was now rendered useless.

The S.O. then pointed out that they have video evidence of the whole incident if they would care to view that, they asked him to show them and he ushered them all into the camera room and played the tape for them,

"I'd keep this safe for the coroners court, said the Detective, it would come in handy as it shows the nurse doing all she can to save them both, other than that it's identifies to us that this is an accident, misadventure on the part of two individuals who never knew they were allergic to anything until now and then it was too late.

The Security S.O. escorted them all to the gate and thanked them, after that he went back to the visits room to have a word with the cleaners but by the time he had got back there they had gone, he looked around holding his head and wondering what the hell he was going to tell his boss,

"He'll hit the bloody roof", he muttered to himself.

Martin called the brotherhood to a meeting in the secret hideout, this was to discuss the latest victim and to inform them all that for the time being there would be no more clients; this was due to the Governor becoming suspicious along with the local constabulary, although there was no way any of the killings so far could be traced back to anyone in the brotherhood he deemed it a more prudent idea to let the dust settle before they embarked on any further victims getting there just deserts.

Although the brotherhood would not be carrying out any other killings this did not preclude them carrying out the selection process for the next victim to receive punishment and planning who, how, where and when it could be carried out.

That evening Martin met Imee at the Midland Hotel, he walked up to the front desk carrying a large package, immediately the receptionist asked one of the bell boys to assist him, he turned and thanked the young lad but stated that he would be fine,

"I have come to meet Mr Rosenberg",

"You are sir", said the receptionist,

"Mr McKay",

Just as he finished Imee walked up behind him and took his hand and shook it, "Martin how are you? Please come with me",

And he led Martin off down the hall and into the lift,

"We will be more private in my suite", said Imee,

They got off on the third floor and Imee led the way to his room, he opened the door and ushered Martin inside, once inside he offered Martin a drink and the two of them sat down, Martin placed the package to one side.

"How can I help you, you sounded very enigmatic on the phone?"

"I wonder if you could sell this for me, said Martin pointing to the package,"

"Well let's see, shall we,"

Martin carefully unwrapped the package, Imee's face lit up when he realised what it was, looking at Martin with disbelief he said,

"Are you sure you want me to sell this beautiful picture,

"Yes I am," said Martin pointing to the "Sunflower painting by Van Gogh, do you think you can handle that for me, you can have one percent of the sale price",

"Five percent, said Imee,

"Now don't get greedy on me, two percent,

"I'll settle for three no less",

"Ok your on, three percent it is, now I need you to do some other stuff for me, with the proceeds I need you to set up a trust fund from which I can secretly donate monies to anyone I wish to, can you do that for me?"

Imee thought for a while still looking at the picture in pure disbelief that anyone would want to sell such a master piece for money, then in the distance he heard his name being called,

"IMEE are you alright, did you understand what I have just said,"

"Sorry" said Imee "can you repeat it, I was miles away",

Martin repeated his request and then the two gentlemen shook hands and went to the restaurant for something to eat, on Martin of course, "your rich!" said Imee,

Martin laughed as the entered the restaurant, if only he knew, thought Martin I still go to work at the prison, I live in the same house, drive the same car and still pay my mortgage out of my wages not bad for someone who is supposed to up with the richest men in England.

After the meal Imee informed Martin that the sale would take a few months so as to get the best offers and he would also need the authenticity paperwork, Martin went into his inside pocket and produced the necessary paperwork and gave it to Imee, both men then hugged and Martin left him and the painting and then drove home passing the prison as he did so, he looked up and could see the cell windows, he turned and said,

"Sleep well gentlemen for one of you will soon be sleeping permanently", and smiled.

Chapter 11

After two months Martin called the brotherhood to order, gentlemen have we decided on our next victim?

"Yes", they all said in unison,

"Then please inform all of us of the name of the person you have chosen",

Stephen Leedery he was a drug lord until they arrested him for possession with intent and supplying drugs, he would have got twenty years but he nobbled the witnesses and the only evidence that the jury had to go on was the video evidence from the police and that was weak to say the least, that was until a young lad stepped forward and gave evidence against him, he was found guilty and given five years, but the young lad went missing and they think that he is now holding up one of the motorway bridges between here and Liverpool the poor bastard.

Leedery has asked for an appeal against his conviction and sentence and it looks like he could be getting a walk out because the kid is missing, we all feel that he should pay for his crime a damn sight more than the judge gave him.

"Good", said Martin,

"Now how, where and by whom",

Albear stood up and then proceeded to explain about his greenhouse and the exotic plants that he had brought from a firm based in America, along with all the strange and wonderful plants was a Aconite, This plant was poisonous but the root is highly toxic and half a teaspoon of a tincture of aconite root placed in a alcohol based drink like whisky or vodka would be enough to kill a very large man. Aconite according to the books that I've read was called "the perfect poison to mask a murder". It can only be detected by sophisticated toxicology analysis using experimental equipment that is not always available in local forensic laboratories.

"Fine but how do we get Leedery to take the poison", said Martin,

"Well," said Albear, "we know that he likes to have a drink, as Jaymo has told us he has been caught with loads of hooch in the past, how about we give him one of them miniature bottles of whisky like you get on a plane, leave it in his cell for him at night like we did for Mac with the heroin but this time it will be whisky, the only thing that we will have to ensure is that AJ is on duty so that he can recover the little bottle and destroy it"

Martin took on board what Albear had said before he replied,

"Good but I don't want any of the brotherhood to be involved in the discovery of the body, the first one was bad enough, so how about this, how long before the poison kicks in and Leedery is at the point of no return",

"It will take effect within ten to fifteen minutes if being digested, before it gets into the blood stream and then it's good night Vienna,"

"Right so Jaymo you go on the wing and give him a spin as soon as he takes the drink, if he is as bad as you say he will down the drink rather than give it up", said Martin.

Everything was set up for Saturday evening, Albear left the bottle in Leedery's cell for him to find, which he did after coming back from the shower, as soon as he saw it he put it under his pillow, just as he did Jaymo walked in and told him that they were locking the wing down and carrying out cell searches and his would be the first and then left.

On his way back from the shower he now realised that on-one else was out on the landings, at the time he never gave it much thought but now he was thinking that this could be a set up, if they find that bottle I'm going to be nicked and taken to the block, he lifted his pillow opened the bottle and drank the lot, unbeknown to him Jaymo was watching the whole thing though the spy hole in the door,

"Bingo," said Jaymo,

He burst into the cell grabbed the bottle out of Leedery's hand and put it in his pocket,

"Your too late I've drank the evidence, so you don't have a nicking",

"What the hell are you talking about? What bottle?" said Jaymo,

Leedery looked at Jaymo bemused at what he had just said, but as the other staff had just arrived he said nothing, he just looked at Jaymo,

"Take him to a sterile area and search him," he said, pointing to two young staff, "you two search the cell and be quick about it we have another thirty to do before we go home, so just a quick glance and check the drawers ok",

"Ok," they both replied,

A few minutes later they returned Leedery to his cell and locked the door, Leedery lay on his bed and began to laugh to himself,

"Dick heads they never found anything, and that other knob has just left with the bottle",

He never got to finish his laugh because before he knew what hit him he was dead, Jaymo ditched the bottle in one of those bottle banks on the way home and as he did so he smiled to himself remembering the look on Leedery's face when he put the bottle in his pocket, to think I would give any of these anything to make their lives more happier what an idiot.

The following day Leedery's body was discovered and the Doctor had confirmed that he had died of a massive heart attack, not surprising considering the life style he used to live and the amount of hooch he had consumed whilst incarcerated.

At the brotherhood meeting the following week Martin and Jaymo went though the incident involving Leedery and the outcome was a success,

"Yet again gentlemen we the brotherhood have upheld the rights of the victim and provided a sentence that is appropriate to the crime well done and thank you, just going off at a tangent do you all and your families have passports and are any of you allergic to the sun, if you could give Jaymo the answer to both of these questions it would be much appreciated," said Martin

Jaymo sat at the end of the table and the brotherhood filed past giving Jaymo the answers, if they didn't have a passports they were told to get one as soon as possible so that the holiday could be booked and paid for, they all turned and looked at Martin and in unison said,

"What holiday",

"Well I was hoping that we could all spend two weeks in Spain not together but one after the other, you decide amongst yourselves when and I'll sort out the payment and bookings."

They looked at Jaymo and rushed to give him the information, after they had finished and gone on their ways Jaymo came over to Martin and said,

"What's going on, how are you going to pay for all of this, are you rich or something?"

"Well actually I am rich; in fact I am one of the richest men in England, thanks to a benefactor",

"You don't mean old Charlie, do you",

"Yes he left me an absolute fortune and that is how I am funding all of this, but you can't tell anyone, and I mean anyone",

"Does Ann know?"

"No, and that is how it's going to stay, until I'm ready to tell her and the girls, OK!"

"OK", said Jaymo as the two of them walked off down the tunnel together, "Well you can buy the bloody shandy's then", he said,

As they walked into the pub Martin gave Jaymo the money as he had to make a phone call, he went to the public phone and rang Imee,

"Hello", said Imee,

"Imee its Martin how'd it go at the auction?"

"Are you sitting down, the painting sold for just over twenty five million pounds",

Imee listened for the reply but there was nothing the phone was silent,

"HELLO", shouted Imee, "Did you hear me"?

"Oh my God! twenty five million",

"You actually get twenty four and a quarter million after I take me fee off it, not bad for a days work, now said Imee what do you want me to do with your money",

"I want you to put five million into three trusts run by the Maahes Trust and Savings Co and the interest from these will be paid equally to Victim Support, Victims of Crime and The Victims of Rape and Sexual Abuse centre, the rest I will be in touch about so just put it into an account and send me the codes to access it at any time, there are some things I need to buy,"

"Will do and if there is anything else I can help you with don't hesitate to call," said Imee.

He walked back to Jaymo looking in a state of shock,

"What's happened, said Jaymo you look as white as a ghost,"

"Nothing I have just decided to purchase some villa's that I've been looking at on the internet recently and after that phone call it will be sooner rather than later.

Martin had done his homework and he purchased three properties in Spain all of which were villa's and then two properties in Portugal and finally he purchased a property in Kissimmee in Florida all of these would become assets in the Savings and Trust company and any time a member of the brotherhood could request to use it, a ticket for them and their family would also be sent to their home address as well as the confirmation form and this would cost them nothing, at any time it wasn't in use the property would be rented out to Joe public so as to look more legit, the total cost of all of these properties was three million pounds.

When he rang and told Imee what he had done and what he wanted him to do, Imee passed him a bit of information that shook him to the core,

"I have just been told to keep my distance from you and someone called Jaymo as the Police are looking to charge you two with four murders, currently the investigation reports have been sent to the CPS for them to decide whether or not to proceed and arrest and charge you with the offences so watch your back and if there is anything untoward going on keep my name out of it do you understand",

"Will do Imee and thank you",

Two days later Martin called a meeting of the brotherhood and told them that he had received some information that they could be under surveillance so he decided that they would have a cooling off period during which time they could enjoy the comfort of the trusts villa's in Spain, Portugal and Florida when he was sure that things had settled back down he would call on the brotherhood to again take up the quest, he closed the meeting and they all dispersed except for Jaymo who he had asked to remain behind.

Martin told him about his conversation with Imee,

"Now is there anything that can tie either us or the brotherhood to any of these killings",

Jaymo sat there and went though every killing meticulously there was nothing out of place that could lead anyone to them,

"There is no way they can tie us to any of the killings, I've been through all of them",

"So how in hell had they got us for this, what are we missing?"

The two of them went over every thing over and over again until they had had enough; Martin was the first to speak,

"Right so lets do it their way then, if the worse comes to worse we will hire the top lawyer in the country to defend us

and leave it to him, if and or when we are arrested we say nothing until our lawyer is present agreed",
"Ok",
Let's hope the cooling off period knocks them off the scent.

Chapter 12

During the brotherhoods lull in any illegal activities the Prison service in its infinite wisdom brought in what was called local recruitment, due to this brainwave it allowed people of a less than favourable background to join as they no longer had to endure the scrutinising that the nationally recruited officer did.

Initially they attempted to conduct the interviews and the selection process the same as previously but after the first few intakes this fell by the way side and then no longer did you have a panel of Senior members of staff grilling you on every twist and turn of your life, the only thing that you had to complete was an application form, take a Test in general Maths and English and do an Awareness test, all of these were completed at a nearby college and then after that in the local Training schools attached to the Local Prisons.

After you passed the tests you then had to complete a JSAC (Job Simulation Assessment Centre) this required the candidate to carry out different scenario's these would have nothing to do with working in a Prison, as someone felt that it didn't require you to be able to carry out daily tasks within a prison.

Anyway you had to deal with four or five similar scenarios and whilst this is going on you are being filmed so as to gauge your actions and reactions to the different scenarios.

Then you get invited to a physical and medical after which a CRB (Criminal Records Bureau) and as long as you have not committed any serious crimes then approximately 6 months later you get your local recruitment posting.

Whilst all that was going on the Police decide that they would put an Operation together to smash the gangs and to remove the guns off the street along with these violent criminals.

Many of the gangs leaders were arrested and imprisoned, so to ensure that they never lost control of their empires the gang bosses had to come up with an ingenious idea and plan which would enable them to remain in control and also to ensure that their orders were followed without question.

There were only three gangs in the Manchester area that had the finances and the resources to carry out this operation in such a way that it benefited them in every aspect, allowing gang leaders who were incarcerated to carry on giving orders and running their massive empires whilst being above the law and bullet proof with regard to charges as they were deemed not able to run their empires whilst locked up.

On "A" wing at HMP Patricroft one of the new young officers was explaining how he became an officer to a little gaggle of prisoners during evening association, feeling really proud of himself having all of these hardened criminals listening to his every word, little did he know that amongst them certain individuals were listening only because they had a more sinister plan brewing.

Although they never acknowledged each other the three main gang leaders were amongst this little group of cons along with their Joes (insignificant individuals who would do anything to please the big boys so to speak), these three had decided separately that they would come up with a plan that would keep them in touch and in charge of their own gangs and that it would be more financially viable for them to have some assistance within the Prison to assist any of their members deal with their incarceration with the minimum of fuss and still be able to run their gangs whilst inside.

Local gangs like The Manx predominately Black members who also had splinter groups who run other areas within Manchester. The leader of this group was Mervin Johnstone he had been brought up in the area and had been in the gang from a youngster, he started by selling drugs and running for the other members as time went on he moved up the command ladder quickly by showing he had the balls and the brains to take out rivals and also any competition he thought may hinder his progression to becoming leader some day.

At the age of 23 he had taken charge of the gang and no-one challenged his orders or authority well not without suffering the consequences at Mervin's own hand, in 1993 he was convicted and found guilty of the murders of two rival members who attempted to take over his turf. Mervin made an exhibition of the fact he was going to murder them to show any other young pretenders that they would suffer the same fate as these two, unfortunately for Mervin the Police had the whole incident on tape as they had him under surveillance for something else but taped the murder of these two sorry individuals.

Mervin on the advice of his solicitor pleaded guilty at the first opportunity and was given a 22 year sentence, during his time on remand he came up with a cunning plan to enable him still to run his empire from within the prison estate.

His second in command and his main enforcer was called Tyrone Malcolm nick name T.M., TM had been with Mervin since Junior School these two ruled the roost and what ever Mervin said went or first of all T.M. would give you a slap and at 7 years old T.M. was a good 5 footer and built like the proverbial brick outhouse and when he smacked you, you stayed down until he left if you knew what was good for you. T.M. was loyal and kept everything running smoothly awaiting the return of Marvin, on a visit to the prison Mervin told T.M. his plan and wanted T.M. to initiate it straight away, to ensure that within six months his plan would be up and running, Mervin told T.M. exactly want he was expected to do and told him not to deviate from want he was told, if one thing was for sure T.M. would do exactly what Mervin told him to do!

The Roses gang were predominately White members who also had splinter groups within other areas of Manchester and Preston). Paul Manchester was the leader of this crew along with his brothers Steve and Ralph, Paul was the brains, Steve was the Supplier what ever you needed from guns to a stapler he would get it, Ralph was the enforcer a black belt in Karate, Jujitsu and Kung Fu he never seemed to smile, there was no emotion on his face but he was always in full control of his faculties never lost his temper he was the iceman of the crew.

Unfortunately in 1995 Paul was arrested with drugs, heroin to be exact, with a street value of two million pound; he was arrested when his drug supplier a Paul Hubble had decided to steal both the money being paid to him by Paul and the drugs.

Paul had sent one of his trusted soldiers with one hundred thousand pounds to pay Mr Hubble, but had failed to contact Paul for over two hours after the purchase time, to cover his arse Paul had sent another couple of soldiers to discreetly watch the transaction taking place, Paul rang his watchers to find out what was going on and was told that his foot soldier had just been killed by Mr Hubble and they had followed Hubble to a local hotel, Paul turned up thirty minutes later with Ralph in tow, he was carrying his little bag of tricks, no-one dared to ask him for a look inside just in case he decided to show them for real, his men told him which room and then stepped back at Paul's request, him and Ralph would sort this trash out. Both walked into the room and a few minutes later Paul walked out with the drugs and money got into his car and drove off, his men remained there waiting for Ralph, after some time Ralph came out and they all got into the people carrier and drove back to there HQ.

Ralph was a bit concerned that Paul hadn't got back before them so he rang his mobile number with no joy, the phone rang in the office and Steve picked it up, it was their solicitor,

Paul had been arrested with the drugs and was looking at a lengthy sentence.

The local press arrived at the hotel after a tip off from there Police informer, he told them where to go and which room, when they arrived the photographer rushed in and started snapping away at anything and everything before he was ejected by two burly officers, the Detective in charge came out and spoke to the reporter, this is a murder enquiry and we will be giving out a statement at the press conference later and until then no further comment. The reporter and the camera man walked back a few steps so that they could see the photo's that he had taken, the female reporter started being violently sick, she had never seen anything like it before, it looked like the man had had his throat cut and then his tongue pulled through the opening and all of his fingers had been removed and placed in his mouth so that the bloody ends protruded outwards, "who the hell had done such a sick and vile act of butchery?" she said, the photographer shook his head still mesmerised by the photo's.

Paul on his solicitor's advice he pleaded guilty at the first opportunity at the Crown Court he was sentenced to 15 years.

No one was ever charged with the murder and no witnesses ever came forward, so the case was left unsolved and still is to this day.

After a few month inside Paul called Steve and Ralph and told them to book a visit, when they turned up he told them of his scheme and what he wanted them to do, and he expected this to be done within the next six months if not sooner at what ever cost, he also told them to use there ace in the hole and get him to coach his boys and also to have a word with the recruiters and put in recommendations for his boys, the two of them left fully aware of what was expected of them and they would not let Paul down.

The Pennines gang had predominately Asian members who also had splinter groups in other areas within Manchester and Bradford). The leader of this group was Ranjit Ali also known as Spanner; he was brought up in a well to do family and had been given every opportunity to better himself. His mother and father wanted him to be a Doctor or Solicitor, he was neither, but his business empire covered a multitude of firms from Taxi's, shops and prostitutes but his must lucrative business was selling drugs and running his extortion racket. If they didn't pay then burn the bastards out was his motto. His second in command was Khan, people called him Genghis because he was considered a bit of a barbarian and would ensure that you could still work but never be able to run away as he would kneecap his victims.

Ranjit had been having problems with a new family who had a newsagents and had refused to pay for any type of protection as they didn't need it as the four boys and their father could look after themselves, unfortunately they didn't fully understand that the protection money was none negotiable they had to pay it or suffer the consequences, this they did on the 30th of July 1993, Ranjit set fire to their shop with them inside. This was to show the locals that he was in charge and they would do as he said not as they wished.

Unfortunately the Police had been informed by the family that they had been threatened and the Assistant Chief Constable thought it may be a racial attack and he was having none of that in his patch, when the Police looked back at the video evidence the Assistant Chief Constable was horrified to see his own son Ranjit, burning out this family. The Assistant Chief Constable went to his superior and informed them that he would have to remove himself from this investigation because of his sons involvement, Ranjit was arrested and charged later that day he pleaded guilty he was given 16 years. A few months into his sentence he called Genghis and told him to visit as he wanted to discuss something very important, when Genghis visited Ranjit told him his plan and told him to use Mohammed to ensure that the right people were chosen and inform Mohammed that even though Ranjit was incarcerated he could still get to him and his family if he wanted to.

Within six months all of the gangs had at least one member employed by the service and another one being trained.

Chapter 13

Martin received a clandestine phone call telling him to put his personal life in order as he was going to be arrested and charged within the next day or so, and then the person hung up.

Martin called Jaymo and told him to meet him in the hide out, Jaymo arrived and Martin was already there sorting out some items he had left there,

"What's going on?" said Jaymo

"You need to get your stuff together because we are going to be arrested soon, now the only thing is we will have to tell the wives and the kids because this will be in the daily papers and the press will hound our wives and the kids, so we will have to get them out of the way, we can send them to Florida whilst this lot is on and then when it is over let them come back, don't worry about money I will give them enough for everyone",

"What evidence have they got on us",

"Jaymo I don't know but we can't afford to hang around, you need to sort this lot out and ring me to confirm that your family will be willing to go",

Jaymo agreed, the two men hugged each other and then after turning off the boardroom lights, they walked off down opposite tunnels.

The following weeks were hectic for both families they had to get permission from the schools to be absent due to personal family problems and Martin arranged with Imee to have their every need catered for whilst they were out there and any monies that they needed would be given to them via the bank accounts which Imee had set up, before leaving Martin and Jaymo kissed them goodbye and gave their wives the cards for the bank accounts along with the access codes, then they were gone.

A few days later whilst in work both Jaymo and Martin were asked to go to the Governing Governors office as they entered the Detective Inspector read them their rights and charged them with the murders of Michael Lowe, Wayne McBain, Lauren Walker and Harry Morse.

Martin looked at the Governor and said,

"Does this mean we are suspended with pay sir?"

The Governor looked at the two of them and said,

"Of course it does",

The detective put the ratchet cuffs on both of them and then the Security Governor took their keys off them and their I.D. cards and escorted both them and the detective out of the prison. They were placed in a Police car that was waiting outside and they were taken to the local Police station and charged formally.

The two of them were placed in separate cells and interviewed in different rooms both men remain silent, the only thing that they did say was that they wanted their solicitor to be present, this went on for over an hour until eventually their solicitor turned up. Both men were released on bail and told when to appear again, this they did with the solicitor in tow and still they remained silent. The police were at their wits end but the Crown Prosecution Service still went ahead with the charges and on the 12th of December 1993 they appeared in court, they both surrendered to bail and were taken down stairs in the dock to the cell area and given a rub down search and then shown back to the dock escorted by their old work colleagues one of which was Daz he winked at the two of them and clenched his fist to show solidarity and that they were not alone. As the Judge entered the whole court stood up and waited for him to sit before they did, he then let the jury in and swore them in. The prosecution barrister went though the evidence that they had which took a day during which time both men were bailed. The following day the defence barrister gave the jury the alibi for every time the prosecution had given up, he asked for the forensic evidence of which there was none so members of the jury he said all my learned friend has are suppositions and circumstantial evidence, nothing resembling real evidence that my clients had done anything other than their jobs.

The case was now coming to a close and after another day of legal talk the Barristers gave their closing arguments, Martin couldn't understand why the Prosecuting Barrister seemed so weak in his summarising up, the jury were given the speech by the Judge about being fair and only convicting if there was no doubt in their minds, and then he dismissed them.

Jaymo and Martin were taken downstairs to the cells by the dock officers, placed in the cell together and left to sit and wait for the jury to decide their fate,

Martin looked at Jaymo and told him not to worry; they would be back in work in no time and they would have a good laugh about the time they were taken to court and got acquitted of murder and conspiracy to murder,

"Glad you're so positive about everything," said Jaymo,

"Jaymo they have no evidence it's all circumstantial, there is nothing to tie us to any of these murders,"

Just then the dock officers came for them,

"That was quick, they want you both back upstairs the jury's coming back in", one of them said,

The two of them looked at each other and smiled, as they entered the dock from downstairs the Judge came in, straight after him the jury entered filing in one behind the other, Martin and Jaymo attracted the attention of their Defence Barrister he just shrugged his shoulders as if to say that he didn't know why it had only taken such a short time to make their minds up or they wanted to know something that was puzzling them about the case.

The Judge looked at the jury and said,

"Foreman of the Jury have you reached a verdict, the foreman stood up and said?

"We have your honour,"

"Please read your verdict,"

"We the jury find the defendants Not Guilty of all the charges,"

"And is that the findings of all of you,"

"Yes your honour,"

"The jury are free to leave the building and thank you for your time,"

The clerk of the court motioned to the courts jury officer to let the jury out, which she did,

The Judge then turned to Martin and Jaymo and informed them that they were free to go and that all charges were dropped, as they went downstairs there Defence Barrister asked them to meet him in the cell area, they both smiled and nodded, the Court Officers shook their hands and said,
"You know we have to be unbiased but we were all routing for you, good luck," the two of them thanked them for there kindness and then left through the solicitors entrance, were their Barrister was waiting,
"What's the matter is there something we have forgotten,"
"No" said the Barrister "but someone wants to meet you both", he walked off and they followed through all the long corridors, until they reached their destination, on the door it read The Right Honourable Judge Meakin, it was their Judge what the hell was going on. The two of them looked at each other with shear shock and horror on there faces, as the door opened Martin first noticed Imee talking to the Judge, Imee turned towards the opened door but didn't acknowledge Martin at all.
"Your Honour what's going on", said Martin moving towards Imee,
That's when Imee made a discreet gesture with his finger pointing out that they were not alone and he should calm down quickly,

He looked about the room taking a mental note of the face in it, the Detective Inspector, the Prosecuting Barrister, the Defence Barrister had now walked in behind them, the Judge, Imee and a fellow in a Saville Row suit possible MI5.

"Gentlemen please take a seat", said the Judge we have something to tell you that could assist you and save you from any further court appearances"

"We don't understand," said Martin,

The Judge ushered him with his hand to sit down and to listen,

"We are all well aware of what you have been up to, and we agree with it, even though we cannot come out in public and state that fact, firstly let me give you my gratitude because the first of your sentences was dealt out to the scum who raped my wife, so from me and my children thank you,"

"And from me" said the Defence barrister, "because the second one was the piece of dirt who killed my father, so he could get drugs", both of these men grabbed at Martin and Jaymo's hands and shook them fiercely nearly pulling there arms out of there sockets,

"But we never killed anyone", protested Martin and Jaymo, "Its lies we were just doing our jobs as professional Prison Officers",

"Ok what ever you say, it's Ok your safe in here, you are amongst friend's".

The Prosecution Barrister then approached the two of them and shook their hands,

"What's that for?" said Martin

"That Morse sexually assaulted my niece and she has never been the same since, she is still having psychiatric treatment, but for both myself and her parents would like to thank you both",

"Listen, will you please stop now we have done nothing wrong, we are both sorry for what has happened to your kin but these deaths are nothing to do with us, please believe us,"

Imee walked over and took Martin by the arm and moved over to one side as the MI5 man took Jaymo over to another corner.

"The phone call was from the MI5 man, Morse had molested his young daughter and he is here to thank you both", said Imee,

"Imee we haven't done anything" said Martin, "we are Prison Officers and that's it",

"So the letter that old Charlie had smuggled out telling me about you and the brotherhood and asking me to look out for you and to give you every assistance is a lie?"

Imee passed Martin the letter, sure enough it was form Charlie saying that he did know about the brotherhood,
"The old bastard", said Martin, "I'm glad he knew,"
"He knew and he approved", said Imee, now listen to the rest that the Judge has to say please,

Chapter 14

Everyone in the brotherhood had enjoyed a holiday at one of the villas purchased by the Trust and had returned refreshed and ready to return to the quest, Martin had asked them to keep their distance whilst the case was on so that none of them could be drawn in.

Jaymo and Martin now looked at this band of brothers in a different light after the conversation with the Judge and his crew,

"You have a mole within your midst, who has been informing the Police of your every move", said the Judge.

"Who is it", said Martin,

"Now that we don't know, but to assist you the Police knew where you," pointing to Jaymo, "ditched the bottle with the residue of the Aconite in it, that was used to kill Leedery",

Martin and Jaymo sat down they couldn't believe what they were hearing one of their own had turned on them, they looked at each other and mouthed the word "Who", both of them had no idea of who it could be, they had known these people for years.

The two of them stood up and thanked everyone for there concern and there assistance and assured them that they would deal with there problem,

"Just a minute", said the Judge, it ends here, there are to be no more killings, this was a one off, any more and your on your own, we will use the full weight of the law to convict you and your band of brothers, please end it now",

"Thank you gentlemen we will take on board what you have said and that will be the end of it",

The two of them walked out after shaking everyone's hand as they were going down the corridor Jaymo turned to Martin and said,

"Did you mean that is that the end?"

"Is it hell we still have one left to deal with and we also have to find and deal with our mole",

"Good because if you didn't deal with it I would have, we need to find the mole fast, before any of the others are drawn in, we need to get Imee to find out precisely what the informer told the Police. They waited outside until Imee came out and was alone, Martin walked over to him and grabbed his arm and ushered him over to his car,

"Imee I need to know exactly what the guy who grassed on us told the Police, word for word, can you get that for us please",

"I don't need to ask anyone, they gave me copies of the reports, here take them",

Imee went into his briefcase and handed Martin a manila envelope but as he did so he took hold of his arm and said,
"Don't get caught this time and ensure that all of the loose ends are tied up, I would hate to lose such a good customer as you",
"Don't worry you wont of that I can promise you, thanks Imee".

Martin and Jaymo read through the reports and sure enough they had a mole, there was nothing concerning the first killing Lowe but days after each of the others there was an anonymous phone call made from pay phone throughout the Manchester area, the first call was after the killing of Mac with the heroin, the caller told the desk sergeant that some officers had killed Mac and to check the bar code on the syringe as it was from the healthcare in the prison and then put the phone down, when the Police had tried to check unfortunately the sharps box had been emptied and destroyed the day before.
The second call told them to check the VP holding room in the Prison as it had been sprayed with pure nut oil to ensure that Morse would die and finally the last one was Leedery, the caller told the police to check the bottle bank at Netto near to the prison and look for a miniature whisky bottle as

this had traces of Aconite in it and that is what they used to kill him, they checked but never found it.

Martin looked at Jaymo and said,

"I thought that was where you said that you had dropped it, in the bins by Netto",

"That's true but I felt uneasy at the time so I pretended to do that but actually dropped it off at Whitefield on the way home",

"David said something strange at the time because he wasn't on duty that night, but he said I shouldn't have dropped it there, now how would he know unless he was following me and saw me pretend to drop it in there",

"How come they never found the nut oil in the VP holding room", said Martin,

"I can answer that, the day after the boss told the works to get it scrubbed out and painted as the investigating Officer said it was a shit tip, so they did it the next day".

"We will have to be careful because currently we have no idea who the mole is,"

"I can tell you two people we can count out", said Martin,

"Who, said Jaymo,

"Us, so that leaves just four to check out, anyone jump out to you",

"No," said Jaymo".

At the last meeting that the brotherhood had held prior to the lull they had already decided who would be the next victim, he had been chosen by Daz, the victims name is Rob Perriman.

"This piece of crap had carried out an armed robbery in a local Post Office and one of the old lady's picking up her pension decide to be a hero and had a go, unfortunately this shit had punched her to the ground and got away with two thousand pounds, the old lady died a year after the offence so he was never charged with her murder. He was caught two weeks later, some well spirited neighbour had reported him to the Police, saying he was bragging about the robbery, the Police found the money and the balaclava and gloves that he had worn and her DNA was on them, he was only given five years and will be out soon, we feel he should be held accountable for her murder."

"Do we know the old lady's name?" said Martin,

The brotherhood looked at Martin bemused as to why he would want to know that detail, he had never asked about the victims before,

Daz responded, "No it wasn't included in the report, why?"

"No reason just asking", said Martin looking at Jaymo,

The two knew where Martin was coming from; maybe she was related to one of the others in the Judges room.

Martin and Jaymo said that they would do this one themselves, without any assistance from any of the others in the brotherhood, the others seemed a bit perturbed as to why they didn't want any help but agreed to stay out of it,

Martin then called the meeting to a close and told them that he would be in touch as to when they would meet again, but not to hold their breath as it may be some time, he asked AJ to remain behind for a few minutes to discuss his forthcoming holiday.

When they had all left Martin sat AJ down and asked him if he could get them two syringes full of liquid Acetylcholine a muscle relaxant that disables victims, which also dissolves into the blood stream thus ruling out any hope of discovery, it also has a long lasting effect on the victim, allowing the victim to speak in a whisper but not being able to move, eventually it shuts down all of their systems causing death.

"AJ looked at the two of them and said,

"Sure when do you need it by?"

"Next week, but this is between us nobody is to know and I mean nobody", said Jaymo,

"Ok consider it done, mums the word",

Martin and Jaymo sat down and planned when they would carry out the deed, the following week AJ gave Martin the two syringes, Martin took one and the asked AJ to assist him and Jaymo with this one,

"Of course, what do you want me to do?"

"Perriman has iron injections every night because we have found out that he is anaemic,"

"That's right he is, but these injections are to be given before tea, I'll have to ensure that he misses it and then go on afterwards",

We want you to put some of his iron injection in with this and just after tea at bang up we want you to give Perriman his injection under the pretence that it is his iron injection,"

"What about the wing staff?" said AJ

"It's ok because Jaymo will be the only one on the wing because it will be in patrol state; I will come on and come up to the cell with Jaymo after you have administered the drug and finish the job is that ok with you?"

"Yeah that's fine, see you then",

That evening during patrol state AJ came on and went to the cell, as he opened the door Perriman looked like a rabbit caught in a cars headlights,

"You Ok?" said AJ,

"Yes I thought you were someone else",

"Who do you mean",

"Never mind just give me the injection",

"As you wish",

AJ walked over to Perriman who had exposed his right buttock to AJ, he pushed the needle in and injected the liquid into his body, as Perriman winced at the pain, AJ drew the needle back out,

"There didn't hurt that much did it, if I was you though I would sit down on your bed as you may feel a bit dizzy or light headed",

"I never did before," said Perriman just as the drug started to take effect, "oh my God I feel like",

That was all he got out as AJ slowly motioned him to his bed, Martin and Jaymo appeared at the cell door, Perriman saw the two of them enter and started to cry,

"Please don't kill me, please",

AJ, Martin and Jaymo all looked at each other,

"Now how the hell did you know that we had come to kill you?" said Martin

"The officer told me to be careful as you two were coming to kill me, just like the others that had died in here",

"What was the officers name",

"I don't know, but he was about fifty odd and slim and athletic looking",

Jaymo and Martin acknowledge who it was and then moved forward,

"Don't and I'll tell you more, I never robbed the Post Office or hurt that old lady, I was told to pick something's up and to tell the neighbours that I had done the job, my boss Paul Manchester made me plead guilty because I owe him and this would pay off my debt to him, I don't know who did the job only that Paul said he would look after anyone who got time as he had an inside man on his payroll".

AJ looked at Martin and said,

"Is he describing David, is he saying that David is the inside man?"

"AJ tell me about the syringe that we used on Mac, has anyone of the brotherhood asked you about it?"

"Yes, David asked how do we record if any are missing and I told him about the bar codes hidden on the needles, oh Christ no",

"Right there is nothing we can do here he's a goner, clean it up and leave now before anyone else turns up", said Martin

As they closed the cell door the last thing they saw was Perriman crying mouthing the words help me, Martin mouthed back that he was sorry and then closed the door.

That night AJ, Martin and Jaymo decide what must be done,

"Where is David?" Martin said,

"He flew out to Spain this afternoon; he has gone to the villa in the hills for a few weeks rest and relaxation",

"We may have to make it permanent", said Jaymo

"Ok Jaymo get your stuff together and tell she who must be obeyed that you have booked a last minute holiday for you and the kids and I'll do the same, we both go in tomorrow and book leave for a week, any problems let me know straight away as your boss owes me a favour or two",

That night the two of them informed their families and they all started packing, the two villa's were only a few miles away from each other, Martin told Ann he was going to get a hire car so he could take them around shopping but it may take the morning sorting it out as he had forgot his licence, he made it to the car hire firm and the car he had pre booked under an assumed name was waiting for him, he showed them his false papers that Imee had provided for him and then drove off and picked Jaymo up.

Chapter 15

The two of them made good time and were outside the mountain villa within two hours, they went in and there was David in his trunks by the pool drinking whisky.

"Hello David" the two of them said,

"Nice to see your enjoying yourself, is it ok if we make ourselves a drink and join you?" said Martin,

"Sure make me another will you this was nearly empty",

Martin poured three drinks, two Bacardi and cokes and a Whisky and soda, he passed Jaymo a Bacardi and gave David the Whisky, and they all raised their glasses and said "Cheers."

"I'm glad you two got off", said David as he took a big swig of his whisky,

"Are you really", said Jaymo "well thank you and cheers again," they all took another big swig,

"Tell me David, why would you inform on the brotherhood about our activities to the Police, why did you betray the trust?"

David began to look uneasy and stood up, but as he did so he started to feel dizzy and unsteady on his feet and had to sit back down,

"What have you done? What have you given me? guys don't do this I had no choice, after the wife left me I got into serious debt and couldn't find a way out, so I robbed a Post Office that stupid old lady had to be a have a go hero didn't she, stupid bitch! I only hit her once and then I panicked, she didn't move, I told her to get up but she just lay there, so I took the money and ran. That's when the Paul Manchester got involved one of his boys spotted me and recognised me from when he was in prison, he paid me a visit and said he would look after me but I would have to work for him from then on, he got one of his boys to take the fall for me, he was the one you lot chose to kill, I had to warn him he was innocent I was the guilty person not him, I'm sorry lads it just got out of hand",

He then noticed that the pool was coming closer to him, no he was being pushed towards the pool, he looked up and could just make out Jaymo,

"Please don't do this, Jaymo, Martin stop him",

Martin came to the front of the sun lounger and smiled at David as he grabbed the underneath and the two of them launched him into the pool, David could do nothing the drug had paralysed him all he could do was look up and watch his two ex mates standing above him watching him sinking to the bottom.

Jaymo and Martin raised their glasses and took a final swig as David's body hit the bottom of the pool, slowly David drifted into unconsciousness and he was no more.

The two of them cleaned up and wiped down everything they had touched and then left, Martin ditched the car after dropping Jaymo back off and then went to the car hire firm in the village close to him and hired a car, they all had a great holiday and were all refreshed for work on the Monday morning. As they went in AJ spotted them first and handed them the morning paper,

"Have you seen this?" he said,

Passing them the paper Martin read it out loud,

"Prison Officer found dead in swimming pool at Spanish villa, coroner has stated that it was a death by misadventure due to alcohol, no one else was involved",

"That's what they think", said Martin

They all started laughing on their way into the prison gate.

Chapter 16

It was a cold and blustery morning the wind cut into their cheeks and stung, the brotherhood were all in their No1 uniforms for the funeral of one of their colleagues, they had been ordered to be coffin bearers by the Governor, unbeknown to him though David was the member of the brotherhood they had killed for turning on them, he had reported them to the Police and informed the gang leaders within the prison, although he hadn't named any of the brotherhood, he did warn the prisoners and gang members that they would be killed if their names were drawn out for selection by any of the brotherhood.

The hearse arrived and the brotherhood stood to attention, David's ex-wife and children were stood close by and as the car pulled up the undertakers men opened the doors, the brotherhood stepped forward and with their white gloved hands they drew the coffin out of the vehicle, as they all took a step back they raised the coffin onto their shoulders and then turned to face the church entrance, slowly they walked into the church and when they reached the far end they placed it on to the roller table.

The vicar gave his speeches and then the Governor gave his, stating that David would be sorely missed, then to the

tune of "Wonderful Land" by the Shadows his coffin moved forward just as the small doors opened, you could see the flames lapping at the side walls as the coffin then went into the incinerator, once it was fully in the doors began to slowly close, the flames inside grew bigger and more fierce, as all this was happening watched by Martin the unelected leader of the brotherhood he whispered under his breath,
"Burn in hell".

As the people exited the church Martin and the brotherhood were now at the church doors ushering them outside and thanking them on behalf of David's family, that is when Martin noticed him, just in the shadows of the church a small insignificant individual who looked ill, his eyes were encircled in black and looked as though they had sunk into his head, his skin looked clammy.
The suit he was wearing hadn't been ironed or sent to the cleaners in a long time, he started to head towards Martin, as he did so he put his right hand into his inside jacket pocket as he got close to Martin Jaymo grabbed him and ushered him to one side, Martin then moved in and they both picked him up and carried him out of the way so that no-one could see them.

"Who the hell are you? and what have you got in your pocket?" said Jaymo,
"My name is Smyth and I work for a firm of solicitors, I have to deliver this to Mr McKay", looking at Martin he said, "Is that you sir"?
"Yes it is",
He handed Martin the letter that had been addressed to him,
"Who is it from" Martin said,
"A David Hillard, he asked that if he died or went missing for more than six months we were to give this to you, now please let me go I have other work to do",
Jaymo let him go but not before he wiped his hands on his creased up suit just in case the guy had the dreaded lurgy and the slightest touch would contaminate him forever.
"What does it say?"
"Hang on I haven't opened it yet",
Martin opened it with care so as not to rip the envelope and then pulled out the letter and opened it up, it read,
"If you are reading this then I am dead or have been missing for over six months, I hope it's dead I would hate to be holding up some bridge wearing a concrete overcoat and no-one knowing where I was, anyway I know I don't deserve your forgiveness because by now you must be aware that I let both the brotherhood and myself down by telling the

Police what we were up to. Please understand that I had no option. Paul Manchester forced me into doing it because he found out about me committing a robbery on a Post Office and got one of his minions to take the fall for me, but if it is of any saving grace I have a warning for you, there are officers who work at HMP Patricroft who are gang members and are there to look out for their members and to provide them with whatever they need, Marvin Johnstone has two, I don't know their names but one works on B wing and the other in the Segregation unit. Paul Manchester is a bit easier as I trained those two to pass the exams, they are officers Campbell and Kerr and finally Ranjit Ali has two, one on K wing and one in Security, Jaymo should be able to assist you in finding out who these are as they haven't been in that long as they were one of the first on the local recruitment programme.

If you could look after my wife and children and make sure that they want for nothing, I know I don't deserve it but neither do they, once again please forgive me".

Martin and Jaymo looked at each other; Martin was the first to speak,

"Rest assured Jaymo his family have been well catered for and along with his pension they will receive a lump sum from our firm and a monthly income equivalent to his wages and a bit more besides",

"Good I would hate for them to suffer because of what we or he did",

Martin turned to Jaymo and said,

"Right Jaymo we need to find out who these people are and fast, and then we will need their personnel files, can you get them or a copy of them?"

"I will have to weed out the suspects and then from there we will have to do some investigating ourselves, the two he had named will be no problem you can have them tomorrow",

"Right once you have them let me know and I will convene a meeting of the brotherhood again, this time it will be for a crusade to save the prison".

Martin went to the hide out and made sure that everything was tidy and that nothing had been removed or disturbed by anyone, he felt different now and he was glad to be back in this haven, when he was in the boardroom he put all of the files belonging to the deceased to one side for destroying and then proceeded to look through the remaining files and found ones for Paul Manchester, Ranjit Ali and Marvin Johnstone he put those to one side as they would require some special attention and then placed the others away in to the cabinet that Jaymo had brought down with him.

Chapter 17

He opened up the first file which belonged to Marvin Johnstone and began reading it, from a very early age Marvin had been involved in some kind of criminal activity and had climbed up the ranks quickly and had eliminated any competition be it real or perceived rivalry. No one was going to stand in his way; he was vicious, merciless and relentless in his desire to obtain absolute power.

As he was going up the rankings he eventually came across his final hurdle the current leader and crime boss called Leon Richards. Leon had been in charge for some years now and Marvin decided that Leon's reign was now at an end, so after asking to meet him at the local drinking hole, Mervin and his henchmen turned up to be met by Leon's second in command Jess Small. He walked up to Marvin to give him a rub down search, as he got closer to Marvin he moved to one side to allow Tyrone Malcolm a clear shot with his magnum, the shot made Jess catapult back into the table that Leon was at. His two bodyguards either side of him began to draw their weapons but it was too late, the first lost his head to a sawn off twelve bore shotgun and the second gained a hole were his stomach was supposed to be and all this before Leon could stand up to get away. Tyrone grabbed him and physically lifted him over the table and onto the floor in front of Marvin,

"Your reign has just come to an end, you're too weak", said Marvin,

The pub was awash with blood and bits of body, now that would have been good enough for most people but not for Marvin he intended to show all of the locals who was the new ruler in the area, he was going to make an example of Leon.

He took him out to the crossroads just down from the pub and lay his body out in a cross with each of his limbs attached to a car, the cars were pointing down each of the roads that lead off from the crossroads and just to make it extra special Marvin stood on Leon and then motioned the cars to slowly move forward and take up the slack in the ropes, as they moved forward Leon's body raised off the floor with Marvin still stood on his chest, so Leon was now off the road with Marvin on top of him, that's when he gave the signal for the cars to drive off down the roads taking a limb with them as they did so, Leon's body exploded showering Marvin in blood and guts, the sight of him stood there covered from head to toe in his rivals blood and innards was horrendous, he looked like an extra from one of those horror movies, he then began to scream at the on lookers,

"And I liked him so imagine what I would do to you and your families if you ever crossed me!"

With that he got into his limo and drove away leaving the crowd to gasp in shock at the devastation he had left behind him.

The Police knew what was happening as they had already been told by an informer but they left it saying it would just be another gang leader less to deal with; they would pick up the pieces at a later date, little did they know how true a statement that was.

People were questioned but no-one had seen or heard anything and that included the landlord of the ale house who stated that he had gone down to the cellar and when he came back up he was met with the sight of all of Leon's henchmen dead in his pub. The Police took the statements and filed them away along with all of the others that had been killed by Mr Nobody.

At the age of 23 Marvin had taken charge of the gang and no-one challenged his orders or authority, well not without suffering the consequences at his own hand. In 1993 he was convicted and found guilty of the murders of two rival members who attempted to take over his turf, Mervin made an exhibition of the fact he was going to murder them to show any other young pretenders that they would suffer the same fate as these two, unfortunately for Mervin the Police had the whole incident on tape as they had him under surveillance for something else but taped the murder of these two sorry individuals. This time he would not get away with it and the Police would not require any witness statements, they had him bang to rights.

Mervin on the advice of his solicitor pleaded guilty at the first opportunity and was given a 22 year sentence, but he was still in charge of his gang.

Martin placed the file down to one side and wondered how this person could wield so much power over a community from within his prison cell, the fear these people must feel just seemed so unimaginable and incomprehensible to anyone not brought up or living within Marvin's boundary.

Shaking his head Martin picked up the next file Ranjit Ali, the son of an Assistant Chief Constable, he had been raised in an affluent area of Manchester and his mother and father had sent him to the top schools within that area and then onto college, although he was not of a muscular build or heavy set he still instilled fear in anyone who crossed him because they thought he was a psycho and he always had Genghis who was considered a bit of a barbarian, now he was big and built like a steam train and hands like shovels, when he slapped you, you stayed slapped. During their time at college Ranjit began to build his empire which now stood at a business worth more than twenty million, and a yearly revenue of five million, his parents wanted him to go to university but he had no interest in becoming a doctor or a solicitor as they had hoped for. As far as they knew he had built himself a small taxi firm and on the side he had a shop selling clothing, they were unaware that he was a major player in the criminal fraternity within Manchester, who ran brothels, night clubs and an extortion racket on the majority of the local Asian business, money laundering, false papers and drug dealing.

Initially he found it difficult getting people to take him seriously due to the way in which he spoke, he sounded like an upper middle class gentleman and dressed in Saville row suits and even Genghis had a Saville row suit but looked very uncomfortable. These two had been together from an early age and both sets of parents enjoyed the fact that these two looked out for each other, if only they knew then what the local community knew and feared, but because Ranjit's dad was an Assistant Chief Constable they put two and two together and come up with five, thinking that Ranjit had the full backing of the Police and that he could do what ever he wanted to do with his fathers blessing and knowledge, if only the truth were known.

Ranjit had been caught on camera by undercover Police officers setting fire to and killing a family who had refused to pay protection money to him.

The Police had been informed by the family that they had been threatened and the Assistant Chief Constable thought it may be a racial attack and he was having none of that on his patch, so he sent an undercover team of Police Officers who were tasked to video the whole incident and if it in their opinion got out of hand they were to call the cavalry in, unfortunately these idiots left it too late and the family died.

When the Police looked back at the video evidence the Assistant Chief Constable was horrified and rushed out of the room, his staff all laughed as one of the Policemen said,

"He hasn't seen the worst part yet and he has left, must have a really weak stomach, pussy boy".

Little did they know, it had nothing to do with victims, it was the perpetrator of the crime that had made him feel so sick, because it was his own son Ranjit, burning out this family and laughing at their screams.

The Assistant Chief Constable went straight down the corridor to his Superior and informed them that he would have to remove himself from this investigation because of his sons involvement and requested that he be given time off to reflect what he and his wife should do now as his standing as a pillar in the community and at work had now been called into question. How could he not know what his son was up to all that time with out helping him or at least turning a blind eye, either way he should have known better, Ranjit was arrested and charged later that day, he pleaded guilty at the first opportunity due to overwhelming evidence and at his Barristers recommendation, at his trail the Judge gave him 16 years.

The last file that Martin picked up was Paul Manchester he and his brothers Steve and Ralph ran the Roses gang, Paul was the brains, Steve was the supplier and Ralph was the enforcer, this lot were the main drug dealers in the Manchester area, no drugs were sold in Manchester that they did have a cut of, any rivals were dealt with effectively and efficiently by Ralph and his crew.

Within their own area they had other business interests but they mainly dealt in drugs, importation of and distribution.

Unfortunately in 1995 Paul was arrested with heroin with a street value of two million pound; it was speculated at the time that the murder of a Mr Hubble was down to the Manchester's but it couldn't be proved even though the Police at the time had forensic evidence in the room that belonged to Paul, but his solicitor got that evidence thrown out on a technicality stating that Mr Manchester had stayed at the Hotel on a previous occasion and it could have been from that stay.

Due to the brutality of this murder it was all over the National papers the victim a Mr Hubble was found in the room with his throat cut and his tongue pulled through the opening so it resembled a ghastly tie, all of his fingers had been removed and placed in his mouth.

When Paul never arrived back at the gangs HQ Ralph rang his mobile but got no answer, the phone rang in the office and Steve picked it up, it was their solicitor, Paul had been arrested with the drugs and was looking at a lengthy sentence.

Paul on his solicitor's advice he pleaded guilty at the first opportunity at the Crown Court he was sentenced to 15 years.

The local press had a field day as all three major gang leaders were incarcerated at the same time and unwisely they proclaimed the streets free of crime.

Martin looked at all three files and wondered how the hell he and the brotherhood were going to sort this crap out and get some kind of stability back to HMP Patricroft without bringing the long arm of the law down on them, or without the gang members who were outside the prison becoming suspicious and then taking out revenge on the families of the brotherhood, there was a lot of permeations to take into consideration before making any moves to eradicate these boils on the arse of humanity.

Chapter 18

Jaymo turned up with the personnel files of the two that David had trained up and about eight others,

"This is the best I could do I have been unable to break it down any further, we have to now find out which of these are the four other traitors and eliminate them".

He placed them on the boardroom table and spread them out, Martin picked up the files on the two that had already been identified and opened the first one which was Simon Campbell he was twenty four year old and lived in Swinton on the Poets estate, he went to Moorside High School and had achieved no academic qualifications whatsoever. After leaving school he worked on different jobs but never stayed longer than a couple of months, until he got a job as a doorman in a night club called the Absinthe Lounge, whilst employed there he applied to join the Prison Service and after completing all of the checks and passing the exam and interview he was accepted.

Martin looked at Jaymo,

"Is that it? nothing more than that",

"No that's it, and they employed him, it's not like when we joined, no panellists grilling you, they make it so simple for people now",

"Christ that's just asking for trouble, it's getting more and more like those private firms, where the cons run the prison not the staff".

He picked up the other file, John Kerr he was twenty two years old and was born and bred in Swinton also on the Poets estate, he went to Swinton High School and also left with no academic qualifications. From school he worked for a local builder and at night he worked at the Absinthe Lounge night club as a barman.
Martin looked at Jaymo and said,
"We have to go and have a look at this night club, how about tonight. The sooner we check out the place the sooner we will find our answers",
Jaymo agreed and at ten o'clock that night Martin picked him up and they drove to the club as they entered Jaymo put his hand out to Martin and said,
"I'll get these you get the drinks",
"Are you sure?" said Martin",
"Positive",
At that time of night it wasn't that busy but it was still bustling, the two of them walked up to the bar, Jaymo was a little behind and was mumbling,
"Everything ok?" Martin said,

"Yes fine",

Martin ordered the drinks and as the barman was serving them they were checking out the place using the large mirror behind the bar.

Once he paid for their drinks Martin walked over to a booth that afforded them the best view of the club, they could see the main entrance and all the way around to the booths to their right, as they had entered the club Martin noticed an advertisement stating that a group called Bi-Polar Disco were playing there tonight,

"How much did it cost to get in Jaymo?" said Martin?

"Too bloody much",

"It may have something to do with the band that's on, there a popular local group",

"Never heard of them he said, how'd you know about them?"

"Distant friend of the family plays in the group",

"Who the wife?"

"Cheeky git she loves me, she's not distant well not yet, I'm still in the good books, anyway she's tone deaf, her parents paid for singing lessons for her when she was at school and after six months the teacher gave them their money back",

The two of them laughed as they slid into the booth, they sat there for about an hour not saying anything just watching the people and the band, that's when they noticed Steve and

Ralph Manchester coming in to the club they were greeted by the Manager and the bouncers, they walked up the stairs to the office and went in, as the office blinds were open the two of them watched them for a while, that is when they saw John and Simon the two officers they seemed to appear from no where, John walked over to the window and looked out towards the club and eyed up the punters and the band.

Steve Manchester walked over and closed the blinds to afford them some privacy and to stop John's mind wondering from what was happening in the office.

"Right let's move now" said Martin, "if they spot us it could get nasty",

Martin and Jaymo got up and headed towards the exit, once outside they made their way to Martin's car and as they closed the car doors they looked at each other,

"The club belongs to the Manchester's, Christ its true did you see those two as bold as brass", said Jaymo.

Martin nodded and then the two of them sat there and pondered what their next move would be, just then the external door to the clubs office opened and both John and Simon stood on the metal staircase talking and smoking, Jaymo and Martin couldn't see who it was they were talking too, not until the door was closed properly by Steve.

The two of them stayed completely still and didn't start the car, they remained in the darkness and just watched, luckily it was a warm night and Jaymo had opened his window to let some air in, so they could hear snippets of the conversation between these three.

Paul had asked for a mobile phone and someone was to have a visit from his boys and they were to put the frighteners on them for something this person had done to Paul, but who or what he/she had done they didn't hear.

Steve passed each of them an envelope which they both placed in their inside jacket pockets, they shook hands and then descended down the metal staircase, this is where Martin and Jaymo preyed that they hadn't parked anywhere near them or it could get dangerous, luckily the two had parked just below the office staircase entrance, they got into their cars and sped off.

Martin started the car and the two of them drove off, as they were going along Jaymo said,

"How could anyone put their fellow officers in such danger",

"They're not real officers Jaymo, they are the lackeys of the Manchester gang, being an officer is just a minor inconvenience to these people, we are going to have to call the brotherhood to a meeting sooner rather than later".

Chapter 19

The next day Martin called the meeting to order and welcomed everyone back into the fold; he opened up first with a small speech,

"I will reiterate what I have told you on many occasions, if you have any problems, be they large or small then please tell, either myself or Jaymo so that we can at least attempt to sort them out, rather than leaving yourself or the brotherhood open to any type of danger".

"Now to business gentlemen we have within our midst at work, gang members working as Prison Officers, we have identified two so far but we have been informed that there are four others that we have to identify and deal with, all this without bringing any suspicion on the brotherhood as a whole, any of us individually and without alerting the gangs to who we are and bringing their wrath onto us or our families".

He explained what he and Jaymo had witnessed the night before and repeated the part conversation that they had heard about an officer getting a visit from Paul Manchester's boys and asked if any of them had heard or seen anything at work which might shed some light on the meaning of this snippet of a conversation.

None of them had but Albear stated that,

"Officer Abbas had phoned in sick this morning apparently she had fallen over and broke her jaw and had cracked three ribs, not sure if this has anything to do with your guys though but it may be worth checking out",

"Jaymo could you check for us please?" said Martin,

Jaymo nodded and left the room.

Martin turned to the rest of the brotherhood and said,

"We have to now come up with a plan of action that is fool proof and cannot be linked back to us, so it either has to look like an accident or as if another gang has taken them out".

They all put their heads down and tried to figure out what to do next. Martin picked up the files that Jaymo had brought and started to go through them to see if anything stood out; that's when he came across a name that he knew and had just recently been mentioned.

"Officer Abbas" he muttered.

Everyone in the room stopped what they were doing and looked at Martin as if he had lost his marbles. Just then the door swung open, Jaymo entered and exclaimed,

"Officer Abbas".

Martin and Jaymo exchanged glances and Martin began "her name is here"

"She is suspected of working for the gangs", finished Jaymo.

"Christ!" shouted Daz, "you two are like an old married couple finishing off each other's sentences".

Jaymo walked up to the table, leaning forward looking into the eyes of all the brotherhood he stated,

"Paul Manchester has just had one of the rival gang's officers beaten up, so look out for repercussions and reprisals from whomever she works for and I don't mean the prison service. So now we know three of the six, we have to keep an eye on her and see who she visits and who visits her."

Martin scoped the room,

"I need to know who is working and who isn't so as to assess their availability for a stake out."

Daz put his hand up,

"I've just finished nights so the weeks yours, but I will need someone else with me"

Albear volunteered, he had booked a week off to go to Scotland but it had been cancelled and his wife was going back to work to save her holidays.

Martin stepped up, "right that's the days covered, the rest of us will cover nights, agreed?"

They all nodded in unison.

"Right let's leave planning anything until we know who we are dealing with, we'll look for the others among these files".

As they did Jaymo set up a whiteboard at the back on a table, he had put pictures of the known officers whom were gang members, along with their names, addresses and which gang they were affiliated to. On the other side of the board he placed pictures of the five other officers suspected to be affiliated with gangs.

Chapter 20

Ranjit had told Genghis to find out who had assaulted his gang member and why, when he visited the girl she told him that they had told her that this was a present from Paul Manchester for disrespecting him on the Wing, she gave him a description of the two guys and Genghis had then told two of his men to check out the Absinthe lounge, the known Headquarters of the Roses Gang and the last known whereabouts of the two remaining brothers Steve and Ralph. One of the gang members that Genghis had sent was Mohammed or as he liked to called Mo a small insignificant looking man who was about thirty but looked like fifteen, anyway whilst they were at the Night club, Mo spotted the two Prison Officers Simon Campbell and John Kerr he didn't know their first names but he did remember their last names and he reported all this back to Genghis,

"So", said Genghis, "These two are working for the Roses gang that's how they got to Helen, those two must have given her address out",

"No wonder they never gave me a touch when I was inside, they were working for the rival gang members" said Mo,

"Well let's give them a little touch, as a kind of thank you for sharing the information, shall we", said Genghis.

The following week at around about nine o'clock at night, Mo followed one of the officers from the prison officers car park and along the A580 known locally as the East Lanc's, when he thought that he was heading for the night club he phoned Genghis and told him,

"Right keep tailing him and if he alters his course tell me straight away, we have a surprise coming", said Genghis.

About twenty minutes later Mo's phone rang it was Genghis, "Is he still in there?" he said,

"Yes boss, but he has just come out of the back door and is about to get into his car",

"Make and model?" said Genghis,

"White Mercedes sports the old type not a new one, he is driving back along the A580 heading towards Swinton", said Mo,

"Ok follow him, but keep your distance you don't want to get in between him and his maker",

Mo looked at his phone and shrugged his shoulders and said "no problem," he hadn't got as clue what Genghis was on about, but he wasn't arguing either, so he kept his distance and followed from afar. Mo could see a massive lorry a few miles ahead of him because he had moved out just a little to give him a good view, all of a sudden there was

a loud booming noise of a lorries horn at the side of him it was another juggernaut travelling at brake neck speed,
"Christ" shouted Mo, "you dick" he shouted at the lorry driver, that scared the crap out of me I thought I was a goner, then his phone rang which made him jump again, he picked it up,
"Keep out of the way idiot I nearly took you out instead of the target",
"Who the hell is this?" said Mo?
"It's me bro, Ali just coming to sort out a bit of road kill for you",
"What are you on about, have you been at the wacky baccy",
"Mo, just stay a bit further back and get ready to slam your brakes on".

Mo watched as Ali who by now must have been doing about eighty miles an hour swing his lorry in behind the officers Mercedes, without slowing down, in fact he just carried on getting faster until he was right on top of the car and with a final burst of speed he pushed the Mercedes under the other lorry that was in front of them, the car was instantly turned into one of those Smart cars but with a humped back, there was sparks, fuel, blood and snot all over the road.
Mo began screaming as he slammed on his brakes and then closed his eyes hoping that no-one would hit him from

behind, he slowly came to a halt and then opened his eyes to see the carnage in front of him, a few minutes later he could hear the sirens in the distance getting closer and closer.

The Mercedes was totally crushed between to the two Lorries, the driver had had no chance, by the time the fire engine and the ambulance crews turned up he had been dead some time. The Police interviewed the two lorry drivers and the driver of the car behind who had witnessed everything they all stated that the car driver was going too fast and had cut in between the two lorries so as to enable him to turn left, the lorry behind had then rammed the car into the first lorry turning the car into a pile of metal, the occupant of the car had died instantly.

The Police allowed the drivers to carry on their way and logged the report down as an accident caused by the deceased driver a Mr Kerr.

Unbeknown to the traffic Police these three drivers worked for The Pennine Gang and this was payback for assaulting one of their gang members even if she was a prison officer, she was also Genghis's bit on the side, Helen Abbas had previously been married to an Asian lad and had kept his name, strange as it may seem her ex-husband disappeared shortly after she took up with Genghis.

"They won't pull that one again" said Ranjit after getting off the phone from Genghis and being told that the rat infestation had been dealt a blow by taking out the trash.

Chapter 21

The meeting was called to order by Martin, over the previous week they had had Helen Abbas under surveillance and now it was time for Daz to give his report to the Brotherhood.

"Gentlemen over the past week we have as you know been watching Helen Abbas at her home address, this guy turned up on a regular basis,"

He held up a picture of Genghis and then placed it on the white board,

"Jaymo has identified him as Khan who is Ranjit Ali's number two, anyway we followed these two to a warehouse in Farnworth when we noticed this officer entering the premises," he is called Mohammed Oram he works on K Wing as a landing officer,"

He then placed his photo under Ranjit Ali, below him was Genghis and then below these two he had Helen Abbas and Mohammed Oram,

"This completes the Pennine Gangs and the Roses gangs pet officers according to Dave Hillard as far as we know, no –one else came to light during our surveillance but what did occur was the death or killing should I say of officer Kerr by the Pennine gang, myself and Albear witnessed the accident, this guy stood no chance and according to this mornings papers it states that a Prison Officer was killed on the A580 when his vehicle was trapped between two juggernauts, initial Police report indicates that the car driver was at fault and no charges were to be filed against the lorry drivers.

"That's great", said Jaymo, "I don't mind them killing each other but we still have to find out who's working for The Manx which is Marvin Johnstone's gang and we can't do anything about any of them until we have all of the information, so let's now turn all of our attention on the missing two, has anyone of the remaining officers come to light or does anyone have any suspicions about any of them".

A.J. was the first to speak,

"During treatment the other night I made sure that I was on B Wing which is where one of them is supposed to be employed and the only one who I would say was acting funny was a lad called Bob James, when I told him that Johnstone would not be getting any further treatment because he hasn't attended at the treatment hatch yet again, he informed me that he normally picks it up for him as the prisoner had gone to the gymnasium as he usually did and when I told him that he wasn't paid to be his Joey (slang for

errand boy) and run around for him, he became quite defensive, maybe he is the one"!
"Well how the hell do we check him out, because if he goes into Moss side and we follow him were going to stand out like a pork chop in a Synagogue", said Daz.

They all considered what Daz had said and they all sat wondering how in God's name they were going to put anyone under surveillance in that area, after about half an hour of stupid idea's being bandied around Albear came up with the first usable idea,
"A detective agency, you tell them you're a jealous husband and you think that this guy is having an affair with your wife, you need him following discretely for a week or so and everyone he meets you want photographing and a report, you'll pay by cash and everything is to be sent to a P.O. Box, once the job is complete there will be a little something extra for their discretion as long as they are discrete, any deviation from the job requested will mean forfeiture of the generous bonus".
"Good idea and if we have a few P.O. Boxes we can send the mail from one to the other by using strangers, for monetary gain of course", said Martin,
"What the hell are you on about", said Jaymo,

"Listen we go to the P.O. Box but we don't open it, we don't even go in, we watch from afar, what you do is pay a complete stranger a few quid and ask him to go in and get the mail and then he takes it to another Post Office and forwards it to another P.O. Box, therefore eliminating anyone finding out who we are", said Martin.

"Right then that's agreed that's what we will do, does anyone know of a Detective agency around these parts", said A.J.

Daz came up with one that his friend had used a few years back, they were good and trustworthy, "they were called K.R. Detective Agency and were located in Hulme just near to Moss side and yes he is coloured so he will blend in better than us, I'll get his number for you and you can start the ball rolling, the sooner we find out who were dealing with the better for all concerned." Just one thing though I personally know the owner of the agency we were in the forces together so at no stage will I be able to get involved in the setting up of this deal, I will pick up the mail and everything else just not that ok",

They all agreed that it would be better for all concerned if Daz kept out of it. The next day Martin phoned the Detective Agency and passed the details of what was required along with the instructions regarding where the reports and the pictures were to be sent, Bob Richards who was the chief detective for the agency took the call and after listening intently he accepted the case and then explained the cost for the investigation per month, Martin agreed the terms.

"Well" said Bob "as soon as the first months payment is made we will begin the investigation".

Martin told him that the money would be in his hand by noon today; Bob thanked him and put the phone down.

"Put the kettle on Mark we have another case and this one pays cash, thank goodness",

At 11:30 that day a courier pulled up outside of the Detective Agency and took a package inside. Samantha the receptionist signed for the package and took it to Bob, he ripped it open inside was a photograph of the suspect a time table of his possible whereabouts for the next two days plus the cash as promised.

"Mark get your act together, the man was true to his word, money, picture, name and a time table, you take the first shift and I'll relieve you later on tonight",

Mark picked up the photo, time table and his wages for the last week and then made his way to the Prison as the target was still on duty, thirty minutes later Mark was in place, he had a good view of the Prison exit, he picked up the photo and took a long look at it and then turned it over and read the name on the back,

"Bob James", he said, "No never heard of him",
He then placed the photo in the file on the passenger seat and now it was a waiting game.

At 16:30hours Mr James was spotted leaving the Prison, Mark photographed him and then set about tailing him from the prison all the way to his home address, he pulled up outside the house and phoned Bob to inform him that he was now located outside the targets house. There was a few comings and goings from the address all of whom Mark photographed and logged the time and duration of the stay, at approximately 21:00 hours the target left his home and headed towards Moss side, Mark kept a discrete distance so as not to alert him, using his hands free he rang Bob again this time to tell him they were on the move heading towards Moss side, Bob told Mark to call him when he was stationary and it looked like the target would be remaining for some time, as he was on his way to Moss side but didn't want to be chasing him all over the place, Mark rang and told him where he was and it looked like the target was going to remain here for some time as it was a drinking den, Bob told him he would be with him shortly and then hung up.
About ten minutes later there was a tap on the window and Mark opened the passenger door of his car to allow Bob to

get off the street and look less conspicuous and of course he had Marks burger and fries in his hand,

"No milk shake?" said Mark,

"I got thirsty; anyway it tasted like ice cream that had melted",

"That's how it's supposed to taste, have you never taken your kids for a burger and fries you mean bastard",

"No they eat proper food, lovingly prepared by their mother",

"You miser",

"Shut up and tell me what's going on here",

"Right the target has entered the house but this is one of those drinking dens for the brothers, I did notice that Marvin Johnstone's number two and some of his cronies have gone in",

"Did you photograph them?"

"Yes but I don't think our man will be interested in those people, do you?"

"He asked that all photo's of the people that this target interacts with are sent to him and that's what we will do, send the lot, he can sort out the crap not us, understood?"

"Yes sir,"

"Now start snapping bro".

When the news about the death of John Kerr reached Paul Manchester and he heard that he was killed by Asian lorry drivers he began to wonder if this was gang related and that it was the beginning of a turf war, he told his brothers to stamp it out straight away and that they should send a message to the other gangs that although Paul was incarcerated he was still able to control his own interests and that they were to find one of his rivals members and make an exhibition of him to make sure that any other rival gangs got the message loud and clear.

Mohammed Oram lived in a predominately Asian community and had done so since birth, his family had moved to Manchester from Birmingham he had been recruited by Genghis at the age of twenty to carry out as he put it a very important job for the community, nobody knew he worked for the local gang leader they just knew he was a prison officer. This station held little or no respect in his community and his parents had requested that he leave the service and take up a more honourable profession, he declined their requests and asked that they respect his wishes, both sides agreed to disagree.

Anyway on the evening of 25th of October 2003 the celebrations for Eid began, this was to celebrate the end of

Ramadan, Mohammed and gone into his local shop which throughout the day had been doing a roaring trade due to the celebrations, he went in for some groceries and as he made his way to the till two armed men burst into the shop and threatened the shop owner and his son, Mohammed froze with his hands held high, the two masked men ordered the owner to empty the till into the bag he had just passed him, just then the owners son grabbed at one of the gunmen, there was a struggle and the gun went off, Mohammed fell to the floor with blood streaming from the gaping wound in his head.

The two men made off without the money and the owner and his son rang for the Police and an ambulance, it was too late Mohammed was dead, the Police told the newspapers and the local television station that this was a robbery that had gone wrong and they were asking the public to assist them if they could to apprehend these two murders.

The two men who had just robbed the store were now a few streets away and getting into their car which had been stolen three days ago, as the men got in they removed their balaclava's and looked at each other and started laughing,

"It went well, it took that kid long enough to grab the gun, I could have passed him the damn thing", said Dean,

"I know, what would you have done if he hadn't grabbed it", said Colin,

"I would have just had to plug the bastard, when the boss wants' someone dead it's either him or me and I know it's not going to be me",

They both laughed again and then drove off slow so as not to draw attention to themselves, when they reached the local country park they drove into an area which afforded them some privacy and then after tossing in their gloves and balaclava's they set fire to the car and then walked off to their car which had been left close by, the two of them drove off and left the car to burn away all the evidence which would link them to the murder.

On Pauls next visit which happened to be the day after the killing he was informed as to the sad demise of Mohammed Oram. He was overjoyed with his men and the result meant that it could not be tied to any of his gang by the Police but the word had gone out that this was a warning to others, who mess with the Roses Gang Members,

"Pass my thanks on to the lads will you Ralph", said Paul "and give them a little bit extra for their trouble,"

"I will do bro, is their anything else outstanding?"

"Not sure how true this is but there is a rumour going round that some kind of brotherhood is involved with the disappearance and death of some of our friends in here, now if this is true I need to find out who they are, where they are and what they know, speak to our acquaintance in the Police and ask him to find out if it is true, and if it is I need to know who their leader is and where he lives, so that we can pay him a visit and either convince him to assist us or terminate this thorn in our side before it gets any bigger."

The following day Bob had the film developed and then went through them discarding the one's that were out of focus or blurred, he then placed them into an envelope with his report and took it to the Post office and sent it off first class,

A few days later Martin picked up the first lot of photographs and the report from the P.O. box, he took them to the hideout and waited for the rest of the band of brothers to turn up, first was Jaymo and then slow but surely the rest followed, as they came in they grabbed a stack of photos and began going through them to see if they noticed anyone they knew, the majority of them recognised Genghis, Marvin Johnstone's number two and some of his cronies but only because they had visited Marvin or had previously been incarcerated, suddenly there was a shout,

"Got one, you little shit, this guy works on my Wing", said Albear,

"He's called Shaun Carter, as officers go he's not bad, we may have to take a closer interest in his activities at work just to make sure, because I would hate to make a mistake about any of these officers",

"Why in Gods name would he be going to a drinking den frequented by gang members if he wasn't part of the fraternity. Can we ask the detectives to watch this guy now as well as Bob James?" said Albear,

Martin answered him,

"No, we will ask the detective to still keep watching and photographing James and lets see what comes from the next batch of photo's, I think we are all in agreement that he is up to no good, just by looking at these photo's it tells you what?" he held up a photograph showing Bob James and Genghis shaking hands outside the club and then another showing them entering the club with Genghis's arm over Bob's shoulder the both of them laughing and smiling, "but as for Shaun Carter he may have been invited there by the James and it is purely innocent him being there."

They all agreed, Albear and Martin would take a special interest in Shaun Carter at work and ensure that at least one of them had him under surveillance at any given time, Daz agreed to assist them whenever he could, everyone said that the detective could keep watching Bob James just until it was proved positive that he was working for the gang either with photographic evidence or by his own confession which was doubtful.

They would wait for the next batch of photo's and see if they could shed more light on whether or not these two were working for the gangs, Martin sent word that the detectives were to continue watching Mr James until told otherwise and to carry on photographing him and any of his associates.

Mark and Bob continued to photograph everyone and sent the reports on a weekly basis, after three weeks a courier turned up with the next months pay along with a request for a different target to be followed and photographed Shaun Carter. When Bob told Mark what was now expected of them, he asked for a meeting with the client.

"We need to see this guy in person, so we can assure ourselves that he is being up front with us and it's not anything dodgy",

"I agree" said Bob,

They had kept copies of all of the photograph's and they decided to check out all of them in one go, as they started going through them it suddenly dawned on them that the majority of these people were gang members and that they could be working for the Police or worse a rival gang.

Bob promised to ask the client for a meeting face to face so that he could satisfy himself that their client was a genuine person and not the Police or a rival gang, and also to put Marks mind at rest.

Jaymo picked up the next batch of photo's and brought them to the hideout, this time along with the report was a note from Bob Richards requesting a meeting to discuss the case further as he was concerned as to where it was going and to ensure that his firm wasn't being used for any illegal activity.

Martin took the note and assured everyone that he would deal with it, this time as they went through the photo's they picked out all pictures with the two suspects in them, Bob James had been photographed with Genghis again outside the club but this time he was putting something into Bob James's inside pocket, stood at the side of these two was Shaun Carter who also had his right hand on his left breast pocket, he looked as if he was laughing with them.

"I think we can now confirm that these two are the last two and they both work for the Manx gang," said Daz "and that completes our board and list for disposal."

Everyone looked at the whiteboard and made a mental note of the officers who would be eliminated for their unreliable service and misconduct to the Prison Service and their fellow officers, all they had to do now was come up with how to kill them without bringing any suspicion on them.

Chapter 22

A.J. came up with the first way of how to eliminate one of them and the only possible cause of death would be that he or she had died of natural causes, everyone looked at him with bemused looks on their faces,

"What?" he said,

"How come you can come up with these unique ideas of how to kill people, it's starting to worry me", said Martin,

"Do you what to know how or not?"

"Please" they all said together,

"Well what we have to do is this……"

He then went into great detail of how this killing would be done, using venom from a Taipan snake; it would mimic death caused by a brain embolism, all we have to do is ensure that it entered the victims body, either by injection or by close proximity to the skin so that it could enter the body through the skins pores the latter being the preferred method, as he was telling everyone Martin was looking through the photo's again, suddenly he shouted,

"How about putting it on his uniform, trousers or shirts which ever would be easiest?" he said,

"Shirts would be better, especially on the collars", said A.J.

Martin held up a photograph showing Bob James going into a Dry cleaner and picking up his uniform,
"Perfect, all we have to do now is find out when he drops off his uniform, when he picks it up and figure out a way of getting into and out of the shop without being discovered or without letting anyone know that we were in there, I've done my part that's yours", said A.J.

Bob James always sent his uniform to the dry cleaners, shirts, trousers the lot, he was a bachelor and as such he did no washing or ironing he would send it on the Friday and pick it up again on the Monday or Tuesday they found all this out by following him for a few times and drawing him into conversations at work he told them quite a few things about himself and his personal life.

Daz and Jaymo had cased the dry cleaners and they closed on a Friday night and then opened again Saturday morning at six o'clock for the early shift to wash the clothes, once this was done then the afternoon shift would do the ironing and leave the clothes bagged and tagged ready for either pick up or delivery on Monday, they were closed all day Sunday so this was their window of opportunity so to speak.

The alarm system for the property was old and didn't work properly so after Daz and Jaymo had set it off twice and the

Police had called out the Manager from his slumber twice he decided to just turn it off and get someone in on Monday to check it out, it was either that or the Police would have charged him for the next false call out they had.

Once everyone had left the area Daz and Jaymo went to work, they climbed in through the upstairs window and then down into the shop at the back, they went over to the racks with the clothes on that were ready to be distributed or picked up and both started checking them looking for Bob James, Daz found it, it was on the delivery rack, Jaymo took the Taipan Snake venom and pasted it onto the shirt collars and cuffs,

"Where does AJ get this stuff from and how does he know so much about poisons? It's scary" said Daz,

"I don't know but I would hate to cross him, one minute your having a nice meal at his house and the next thing you wake up in a coffin after being buried alive, I'm glad he's on our side, anyway this should have dried in by the morning and will be untraceable", said Jaymo,

The whole process took about half an hour and then they were gone without leaving a trace that anyone had been in the shop, they stayed outside all night just in case any local burglars had got a whisper that the shops alarm system was down, they were taking no chances.

The next morning the Manager arrived early and had an alarm fitter in tow, once the two of them entered the shop Daz and Jaymo left, Jaymo rang Martin and informed him that part one of the plan; had been put into action.

Jaymo and Daz pulled out of the alleyway and slowly drove off so as not to draw attention to themselves, they headed towards Bury and the hideout, they had rung Martin and he told them to meet him there and he would take them for breakfast to discuss the next move.

When they arrived at the car park next to the hideout Martin was waiting, they all walked off to McDonalds and Martin went to the counter for the breakfasts. Jaymo and Daz found a booth which gave them some privacy enabling them to go through the night's details without being overheard by anyone.

They told Martin about having to set the alarm off twice and then race back to their car and await the Police and the Manager turning up,

"How did you know that the alarm wasn't set on the third occasion when you went back to the shop", said Martin,

"My brother in law is a Manager of a shop and he had the same problem and the Police told him it was causing a public nuisance and he either turned it off or got it repaired, and because we set this one off at gone midnight the

Manager had no chance of getting an alarm fitter that late, not without it costing him an arm and a leg so we were quietly confident," said Jaymo.

"We ensured that none of the poison went onto our hands or clothes and the gloves and boiler suits that we used are in this bag, Daz picked it up to just above the lip of the table to show him.

Martin took the bag and told them he would be back in a few moments, Jaymo and Daz tucked into their breakfast meal and coffee, it was good, after five minutes Martin returned and joined them,

"We now have to take care that after he suffers the embolism the coroner doesn't check his clothes for any substances", said Martin.

Chapter 23

No-one could guarantee when Bob James would put on the doctored uniform so all of the brotherhood for the next week or so had to ensure that at least one of them had eyes on him whilst he was at work, they didn't have to follow him to work and they didn't need to follow him home from work because once the venom entered the blood stream through the pores which could take up to four hours from initial contact, the victim would start to become very hot and sweaty, then they would begin to feel choked up and unable to swallow or breathe properly, this would then lead to them fighting for breath and then foaming at the mouth, after that death is almost instantaneous, there is no hope of recovery.

Monday morning Bob James was off work and he had his uniform delivered to his house, he laid out one complete set of uniform, for his late shift.
Daz and Jaymo had covered this shift and by the time Mr James had arrived they were both ensconced on the wing awaiting his arrival, throughout the shift the two of them were on tender hooks just waiting for him to drop dead, it never happened and come the end of the shift the two of them followed Mr James out of the establishment, before they got

into their cars they rang Martin and informed him that the first shift had passed without a fatality namely the officer.

The next day A.J. and Jaymo were on duty, when Mr James turned up he was looking a bit flushed and hot under the collar, the two of them looked at each other this could be it they both said together, they followed him all over the prison and then eventually onto A wing just as he was going up the stairs he collapsed and started twitching, both A.J. and Jaymo who were just coming onto the wing and immediately noticed what was occurring, they both turned around and left, listening to their radio's as they did so that's when they heard the all stations medical assistance required as a member of staff was fitting.

A.J. looked at Jaymo and said,

"Should I attend as I am one of the medics on call and it would look more suspicious if I didn't?"

"You go and I'll be with you in a minute," said Jaymo

A.J. made his way onto the wing and arrived just after his other colleague, she was already checking the officers vitals and A.J. began assisting her by undoing his tie and collar, just then Hotel one arrived with the big medical bag which contained everything that a paramedic would need including a portable defibrillator machine, "I'm getting no pulse" shouted the female nurse, A.J. checked she was right, "nothing" he said

"Stand clear I'm going to shock him",

A.J. ripped open the officers shirt thus exposing his chest and then stood clear before the first controlled electric shock was administered,

"Check him again",

"Nothing",

"Clear",

Again he was shocked but still there was no pulse,

"He's gone, are we all agreed?"

They all nodded and then looked at their watches, the doctor turned up and pronounced him dead, and they removed the body to the Healthcare and awaited the ambulance so that he could be removed to the local hospitals mortuary.

Jaymo had been watching from the landing above them and when A.J. spotted him he made a subtle cutting motion with his hand across his throat, that was all that Jaymo needed to know, he went into the office on the landing and picked up the phone and rang Martin,

"Martin its Jaymo", he said,

"It's ok we've heard over the net, see you at dinner", Martin hung up.

A.J. and Jaymo escorted the body to the Healthcare Centre, when they arrived they laid his body on a table in one of the treatments rooms, once everyone else other than A.J. and Jaymo had left, Jaymo took off his shirt and passed it to A.J., the two off them then put the shirt on Bob and took the other shirt covered in venom and placed it in a sealed bag for Jaymo to dispose of.

Jaymo had put his black polo shirt on under his white work shirt just in case they needed it, good job he had, as part of the DST (Dedicated search team) he was now properly dressed and didn't look out of place as this was his normal attire for carrying out his daily duties.

That night the brotherhood met and everyone except Martin was on time, the others began talking amongst themselves as Jaymo was altering the notice board, he first wrote across the face of John Kerr killed by the Manx gang and then across the face of Bob James eliminated by the brotherhood, just then the door swung open and Martin appeared at the entrance to the room, he looked over to see what Jaymo was doing and shouted,

"And across Mohammed Oram's face write, murdered by armed robbers at a convenience store",

They all looked at him in disbelief this was to weird to imagine,

"Someone else is knocking these lot off, other than us", said Daz,

"This would be the second of the six officers to be killed in suspicious circumstances; this is like a two for one offer or the, kill one and we kill one for free".

We need to know who is doing these killings before we end up in the middle of something else, this could be gang related and if they find out about us we could be next for the chopping block," they all nodded in agreement.

"So we know that the Pennines killed Kerr now did the Roses kill Oram in a tit for tat move", said Martin.

"Anyone got any contacts in the Police who could find out without involving the brotherhood?"

"What about the MI5 man, the one whose daughter had been molested by Morse?" said Jaymo,"We could ask him",

"Did you forget that we weren't supposed to be doing any of this after the court case we were warned off",

"Oh yeah",

"Well ask Mike the copper who lives next door to you, he likes to talk shop, if you drop it into the conversation he may let something drop and we can take it from there. Just say that one of your officers at work has been killed at a local shop and see what comes up".

"Ok I'll try but I'm not promising anything",

That night Martin spotted Mike coming home from work and as he parked his car up Martin appeared from his front door and went to his car on the pretence of getting something from the boot,

"Hi Mike how's it going?"

"Not bad, yourself?"

"Not much just that officer who got killed in the local shop, he was from my prison",

"Yeah", said Mike, "strange one that, the investigating officers think it is something to do with local gangs and turf war or something like that",

"But what was it to do with the officer who got shot",

"Nothing, just wrong place wrong time they suspect",

"Apparently the shop is under the protection of some gangster called Ali, he is currently in your place and these people are trying to muscle in on his action or something like that", anyway they have it down to two gangs the Manx or the Roses not sure which yet but they have promised to make an arrest soon, so watch this space".

Chapter 24

After the death of Bob James one of the officers employed by the Manx Gang, Mervin Johnstone had given Tyrone the order that he was to search out and deal with the killer of his man, Tyrone had set his men the task of finding out who was involved, his first clue to who may be involved came from one of the doormen at their drinking den, he had spotted a car that had been outside the club for some time and he recognised one of the occupants of the vehicle as Mark Walsh someone he went to school with but the other man he didn't recognise.

Tyrone told his men to pick Walsh up and take him to the warehouse and to keep him entertained, Mark was sat at home watching his favourite programme NCIS when he heard a knock at his door, as he approached his front door it burst open knocking him to the floor, before he could react two huge giants had him by each arm and flung him up against his hallway wall smashing his face into the mirror which exploded into a thousand shards. His face changed colour with his blood which was now pouring from all of the small cuts that had been inflected by the mirror glass, one of the men threw him a towel which he held to his face.

"Keep it there because if you move it before you are told we will kill you",

Mark muffled his agreement; they bungled him into a van and made him lie on the floor, after what seemed an age they pulled into the warehouse.

"Remove the towel and follow me", said the man,
Mark took the towel from his face and looked at it; it was covered in blood, his blood. Someone pushed him from behind, but he didn't look, he faced forward and did as he was told, these people weren't messing around.
As he was walking he was making a mental note of all of his surroundings, looking for exits, windows, how many men were in the place and where they were located, he spotted three men at the entrance and as he followed obediently he noted the offices along the right hand wall there were two gang members in them, there were lots of boxes and vehicles but he never noticed any other men.
When they reached the end of the building they entered the main office, waiting for them was Tyrone and the doorman, when Mark entered he recognised the doorman straight away,
"What's this about ?" said Mark,
That's when he started hearing ringing in his head as one of the guy's behind him hit him with a rubber cosh, Mark automatically grabbed his head just before he hit the floor,

they picked him up and threw him in the chair which was in the middle of the room, they then tied his arms and legs to the chair, once he was secured, Tyrone walked over to him and grabbed his head and lifted it up,

"Who are you working for, which gang ?"

"I don't work for any gang, I'm a private detective",

"Why are you watching our drinking den then", said Tyrone,

"We were following up a lead, we have been employed by a jealous husband who thinks that one of the men who spends a lot of time at your drinking den is having an affair with his wife",

"Who", said Tyrone,

"Bob James, that's who,"

"He's dead, someone killed him, said Tyrone,

"No-one killed him; he died of a brain embolism",

"Don't you think he was a bit young for one of those?"

"Yes but the coroner said it was a one in a million occurrence in someone of his age", said Mark,

"Who employed you I need a name, now before I have to let this lot loose on you!"

Mark looked around the room all of the other people in the room had armed themselves with clubs and coshes, the doorman had got a pair of pliers and was tapping them in his hand,

Mark looked at Tyrone and swallowing hard he said,

"I don't know who it was, I do all the leg work and all I'm told is who the target is not who has asked us to do the job",

"Well that's unlucky for you then isn't it, you should always know who is sending you into the lion's den, you won't do this again, well not for awhile after we have finished with you and the next time you'll ask the right questions won't you",

"Please don't", said Mark,

Tyrone looked at his men and nodded and then he took a step back, his men moved towards Mark and as the first one lifted his cosh to give him a taste of its leather there was an almighty crash outside, Tyrone opened the office door to see his gang members being held by masked men with guns and a 4X4 heading towards the office with its headlights on full beam and Bob the owner of the detective agency shooting his pistol in the air, the vehicle crashed into the office sending all of the other gang members diving for cover, once the vehicle came to a halt Bob jumped out and headed towards Mark, one of the gang members stood in his way so he pistol whipped him, the guys mouth exploded into a mass of blood, the other gang members remained under cover.

Bob moved fast and cut Mark free from his binds and told him to get in the vehicle, Mark didn't argue and made it to the vehicle in record time, Bob looked around and spotted

Tyrone attempting to take cover behind his desk, Bob walked over and pointed the gun at him,

"Please don't shoot", said Tyrone,

"Not nice being on the receiving end is it?" said Bob,

"Why did you take him? What has he ever done to you?"

"He was seen outside our drinking den and then a few days later one of our friends was found dead, he says that he was being paid to follow him by some jealous husband",

"Now listen carefully, Mark doesn't know anything, he works for me and I own the business and if you would have done your job properly you would have found that out, now if your on about Bob James we were following him but as to who employed us to do that job, the only thing we have is a P.O. Box number which is, and Bob told him the number and the location of the box as he was leading him out of the office and into the warehouse so that he could see the rest of Bobs friends who by now had rounded up Tyrone's gang and had them all sitting on their hands in front of the other offices in the warehouse,

"Now let this be the end of this", said Bob "are we agreed?"

"Yes" said Tyrone, "As long as you keep your nose out of our business in the future, we will call this quits, but you had better ensure that our path's never cross again", they both agreed and Bob got into his vehicle and reversed out, followed by the masked men.

As the vehicle got outside the warehouse the masked men held onto the side of the 4X4 and Bob drove off slowly, so that they could ensure that no-one was following them, No-one did.

Bob pulled up about six streets away from the warehouse and the men jumped off and moved to the edge of the road, one of the masked men approached Bob and removed his mask it was Daz,

"Thanks mate", said Bob,

"No problem that's what friends are for, any way if I needed help you would have done the same",

"Thank your friends from us both",

"Will do, now are you two going to be ok?"

"Yea we'll be fine",

Daz waved the two of them off and then returned to the other masked men,

"Ok guy's they've gone you can take the masks off",

"Thank God for that", said Martin, "It was getting hot under here",

"Too true", said Jaymo, as he removed his mask,

After all of the brotherhood had removed their masks, they got into the van which they had waiting for them and drove off ensuring that they weren't followed, Martin took them on a sight seeing tour of Salford and Swinton before making their way back to the hideout and their cars, once he had dropped everyone off he took the van followed by Albear to a derelict site and set it alight with all of the black boiler suits and the gloves, masks and the imitation firearms inside and to ensure that it all burnt they used petrol with a touch of AVPIN (Iso Propyl Nitrate IPN) a high octane fuel used in Hunter fighter jets, you only need a small amount as this burns well, Albear had got some for his model aeroplanes but it had blown the cylinder heads off them so he just kept it for an emergency, like today.

They waited around but at a good distance until the van had burnt down to nothing more than a shell, the fire brigade crew turned up but as it wasn't life threatening they were told it was a low priority call out, nothing of that nights fun and games was left or could be used to gain any forensics from.

Martin and Albear drove back to the car park and Martin got out and told Albear he would see him tomorrow, he watched him drive away and then proceeded to the hideout, once inside he went to the board room and checked the white board, he would remain there for some time to see if he could make any sense out of the nights proceedings. Why had they gone after the detectives and what had they told them about their client, he would speak to Daz in the morning and ask him to discretely find out from Bob.

That night both Bob and Mark had a heart to heart, when the detectives started to become suspicious about these people that they were following as all of them it seemed belonged to the same gang the detective's decided to request a face to face meeting with their client,

"When he didn't turn up for that first meeting we should have known better then", said Mark,

"We didn't know that this would happen, he did give us another appointment, but because the money was coming in on a regular basis, we got greedy", argued Bob,

"Yes but to allow him to cancel a further four times we must have been stupid as well as greedy", shouted Mark,

"Ok I'm sorry, in future we will be more careful, thank God you are still in one piece",

"No thank your friends", said Mark,

"Amen to that", agreed Bob.

Mark looked at Bob and said,

"Ring Sam and make sure that she's ok and you'll have to tell her to have a week off until we can be sure that that lot are going to leave us alone",

"You're right",

Bob picked up the phone and dialled the number, Sam answered straight away and Bob told her everything and that he would see her in a few weeks and not to worry she would still be paid, he then hung up.

Mark patted him on the back and said,

"You know it make sense, and by the way make sure that bastard pays in full along with his generous bonus we deserve it",

Bob sat down and wrote his last report for the "Client" this time there were no photo's just a request for full and final payment and the bonus that was agreed, as this contract was now terminated forthwith.

The following day Martin had called Daz and asked him to meet him at the hideout as he needed him to contact Bob and Mark,

Daz turned up spot on time as usual,

"What's up, what do you need?"

"I need you to go and ask Bob about last night, I need to know what all that crap was about and if it involved the brotherhood in any way",

"Do you think it does?" said Daz,

"Well he takes us on as a client, all be it unbeknown to him, but the people they are watching, kidnap his employee and then he asks you for help because you two served together in the SAS, now we need to know what they asked them about and if it involved us and also what he told them about us, his clients, do we have to watch our backs because these guys will be coming after us or is that the end of it because he told them something different from the truth",

"I see," said Daz, "I will ask him out for a drink today and get to the bottom of it and then contact you with the information",

Daz left and went straight to his car, he picked up his mobile and rang Bob and invited him for lunch, on him, Bob accepted and the two of them arranged to meet at a Public House which served food and was located just off the M61. When Bob turned up Daz was already at the bar waiting, as he got to the bar Daz turned and shook his hand and gave him a pint with the other, the waitress showed them to their table which Daz had requested be far away from any prying ears, when they sat down the waitress took their order and left them,

"What's this about?" said Bob, "It's a bit clandestine isn't it",

"I need to know just for my own peace of mind, what was that shit about last night and what went down".

During lunch Bob explained everything, Tyrone had asked Mark and him about one of their client's,

"This guy was very secretive and all they had was a P.O. Box, they had been sending all of the photo's that they had been taking to this mail box religiously, and how they would get further instruction and more money each month, everything was going great until last night when those lot turned up on Marks doorstep, luckily I was just outside his house when they went in all heavy handed, that's when I called you for help, when we went to the warehouse I told Tyrone that we had no idea who our client was and that all we had was a P.O. Box number and where we drop it off at, which I gave him last night",

Daz turned ashen, quickly excused himself and told Bob he would only be a few minutes he had just remembered something, Daz ran out to his car and picked up his mobile phone and rang Martin,

Martin answered, "Hello",

"Martin, its Daz, who is going to pick the mail up today",

"It's Albear's turn why",

"Quick ring him and tell him to stay clear it's not safe, I'll explain later",

Daz hung up and Martin rang Albear, nothing it went to answer machine, he tried his house number no answer, so he rang Jaymo who picked up straight away,

"Jaymo meet me at the P.O. Box and if you see Albear warn him to stay away from it, it's not safe, get there now",

The two of them raced towards the office building in Manchester where the P.O. box was, they arrived together and parked up opposite the building, got out of their cars and headed across the road dodging oncoming cars as they did so, but it was too late Albear was already inside, they could see him through the massive glass fronted windows, he was at the box and was about to put the key in and open it, that was when he spotted Martin and Jaymo running across the road waving frantically, he waved back whilst at the same time slipping the key into the lock and turning it, there was a weird whooshing sound followed by an almighty bang and the whole of the front of the office building exploded in a mass of glass shards and flames which flew into the street, the cars that were parked outside the office block were picked up and flung across the street towards Martin and Jaymo, that's when Martin noticed Albear's wife and daughter in the car coming towards him, they were screaming but he couldn't hear them, the next thing he knew was he had been flung to the pavement, and was sat on his backside dazed he looked around and saw Jaymo a few feet away he had the look of both fear and shock on his face, with their ears ringing from the explosion he shouted to him that Albear had brought his family with him to pick the mail up and had parked up outside the office, they were in that car, he pointed to a burning shell of a once pristine vehicle. People were screaming and running around like headless chickens but the sound was muffled and distant, the two of them just sat there in total disbelief at what had just happened to their best friend and his lovely family.

Chapter 25

The Police and ambulance crews were there in quick time, the Police blocked off the road at each end and the ambulance crews started doing triage on the main road, marking out those that were urgent and non-urgent, when they got to Martin and Jaymo they pinned a card to them and went onto the next person. Their hearing was slowly coming back to them, Martin stood up a bit unsteady at first and walked over to Jaymo who was also getting to his feet, the two of them held on to each other and Martin said,

"We need to get in touch with the others now! We are all in danger! "start ringing the others".

The two of them contacted the rest of the remaining brotherhood and told them to get too the hide out fast and they would both meet them there, the two of them walked off towards their cars and then slowly drove off towards the hideout, when they got there everyone was waiting. When the others saw the state they were in everyone started speaking at the same time, Martin held up his hand and they all fell silent and sat back down.

"Albear and his family are dead they were blown up whilst collecting the mail, myself and Jaymo tried to get to him but we were too late",

The room erupted again, with everyone speaking at the same time,

"Quiet", shouted Martin, "One at a time",

Daz was the first to speak,

"Was this because of me calling you all in to assist Bob and his friend", said Daz,

"No we have got sloppy and let our guard down, remember we had a set protocol about picking up the mail, you send in a stranger and pay him to send the mail on to the next P.O. Box not go in and get it yourself and definitely don't take your family with you, also you all need to keep your mobile phones with you at all times when you are not in work and keep them switched on, if Albear had followed just one of these he would probably be still be alive now".

"The only thing is we need to contact John", said A.J.,

"Who is John",

"He is Albear's son who is currently at University in Edinburgh studying computer engineering", said Daz,

"If A.J. knows him I think it would be better coming from him, but before he speaks to him we need to discuss what we are going to do for him, with regards to ensuring that he finishes his studies and that he does not get involved in any of this, because if he is anything like his father he will be out for blood and the last thing we need at the moment is a loose cannon".

Over the next few months everything went quiet. The Brotherhood were in mourning for a lost colleague and the Gangs had decided to keep their heads down so as not to throw suspicion on them, the only good thing to come out of all of this was the growing friendship between A.J. and John, they had become like a family to each other, A.J. the uncle he never had and John the nephew A.J. never had.

After the funeral A.J. and John went on holiday together in one of the Brotherhoods villas in Spain, when they returned John had decided to take up the offer from GMP and become one of the leading new lights in the Police Force, he was also offered a position in Scotland Yard but had declined it, because he wanted to work in the area that he had grown up in and knew so well.

He was a fast learner and soon became the lead in IT and Communications and Programming, he designed and wrote all of the new programmes for the Police Forces and had lead the way in the training of staff.

Nationally he had designed and implemented a new system for the storage of evidence both written and physical this programme was automated and would store and cross reference evidence whenever it came in, against any old ones, any that were highlighted as having similarities, it would send out the evidence on that particular case to the lead detective to peruse.

A.J. became the proud father figure in John's life and the two of them became inseparable, going out at night together and at weekends A.J. helped refurbish and extend the old house that John once shared with his family. Everything was hush, hush and after four months of hard work and graft by the two of them they had the grand opening, well John got the two of them a beer and ordered a Chinese takeaway.

Chapter 26

Martin called the meeting to order, the room seemed more empty than usual.

"Who's missing?" said A.J.

"Daz, where's Daz, is he on duty?"

"Gentlemen, this meeting is to inform you that I received this today",

Martin held up some photographs and a letter, he passed them around the room, they showed Daz, lay seemingly unconscious and concrete being poured over him, the last picture showed the concrete all smoothed out and no Daz.

"What does the letter say?" they shouted,

Martin picked it up and read it out aloud,

"Stop now or you will all end up this way, you have been warned",

There's no name on the letter, so we don't know who it's from, they all sat in silence stunned at what had happened to their brother, now they had killed off two of them, how many more before this was over.

"Do we have any idea where they dumped the body, so we can at least give him a proper burial?" said Jaymo, "were not going to just leave him out there".

Martin checked the pictures and the letter then he looked at the two of them and said,

"What can we do? There is nothing in any of the pictures or the letter to give any indication of where they dumped him".

They all sat in silence for a while and then Martin stood up and walked over to the white board and eyed up all of the pictures of the different gangs, then pointing to it he said,

"One of these bastards knows about us or at least some of us, but how?"

"Someone must have talked, or we have made a mistake along the way and someone has noticed us",

There were only three of them now so they had to make sure that they all remained alive to finish off the last of the bogus officers acting on behalf of the gangs. All the gang members who had been either killed by the other gangs or had been eliminated by the Brotherhood were removed from the board and placed on the table in front, but not before Martin had made sure that everyone was in agreement, he held up each one in turn and checked the back to see what had happened to them.

First one, John Kerr killed in a car crash on the East Lancs by the Pennine Gang in retaliation for Paul Manchester hitting one of his paid officers. Mohammed Oram who was murdered in a pretend robbery that went wrong and finally Bob James who was terminated by the Brotherhood using poison, there's not many left now said A.J.,

"No but just enough to take us three out, we need to start making our move, and ensuring that we cover our tracks better, lets attempt to get these last three officers and see what happens from there, are we all in agreement?

They all agreed now we have to decide how we are going to get them, so how are we going to get Shaun Carter, Simon Campbell and Helen Abbas all together and in one foul swoop take these three out of the equation.

They all sat down and had something to eat and drink whilst contemplating how to get these together, they first just threw ideas at each but in the end it was Martin who came up with the solution to their problem,

"We can send out letters with the P.S.S.A. lottery letter head telling them that they have won either first, second or third prize in the main draw, because checking the profiles that we have done on these three they all subscribe to this Prison charity ",

"What the hell is P.S.S.A.? Lottery", said A.J.,

"The Prison Service Sports Association Lottery is the charity that Prison Officers sign up to in the first year of joining this job or in your case not or you would have known what it was",

"If we send them an invite to a local hotel and then get them to fill in a form stating what menu they would like and what drink they would prefer with that meal and then after that they will be informed as to which prize they have actually won.

A.J. we will need a poison that will paralyse them but not kill them, they must be able to be moved with the minimum of fuss, we can hire a van and bring them here and hold them in the safe room, there are shackles on the wall at the back, we will just have to clear out some of the things in there to accommodate them".

That night Jaymo made up the letters and gave them a P.O. Box number to return the letters too, Martin made sure that the room was cleared out and the items put into storage, A.J. found a poison to facilitate the officers being unconscious but still able to be moved,

"Vecuronium" said A.J.,

"Vec what" asked Jaymo,

"Vecuronium it's a neuromuscular blocking agent, a type of muscle relaxant that is commonly referred to as a paralytic agent. It prevents nerve impulses from the brain from signalling the muscles of the body to move, preventing most of the muscles of the body from moving. The heart isn't stopped it continues to beat after administration of the drug. Martin and Jaymo looked at each other and in unison said," Thank goodness he's on our side", then they turned and laughed at him,

"What?" he said,

They all then continued to go through the list of things to do and as they completed one, they would tick it off the list, Martin ordered and paid for the van and kept it hidden away in a disused warehouse that he had rented for a few months until they needed it.

One week later the letters had been returned and the menu's and the preferred drink requested, Jaymo sent out the invites and the name of the Hotel and the date for the venue, everything was ready, on the day in question they all took up their positions and waited, first to arrive was Helen Abbas, she was shown to her room and left to unpack, all the rooms had been selected for there easy access to the car park at the back through one of the fire exits, next to arrive was Simon Campbell he was shown to the room across the way from Helen and then finally Shaun Carter arrived. He was placed in the room next to Helen, the room facing him was where Martin, A.J. and Jaymo had set up base, before sending out the menu's they ensured that all of the meals on the menu were high in spice or strong flavours so as to mask any after taste of the vecuronium which they would put in their drinks, they were unsure if Helen was a practicing Muslim but when they received her menu back they soon realised that she wasn't, she had requested Gin and tonic with a slice of lemon, good job that the drug was clear in colour she may just think that the Gin is of lower quality then she was used to.

At around about eight o'clock they were all invited to the dining room for their meals, as they all came out into the corridor they all looked at each other and laughed, Simon was the first to speak,

"We'll Helen you do scrub up well", he said,

"You two don't look so bad out of your goon suits", she replied,

Shaun held out his arm for her to take and said, "May I escort you madam",

"You may", she said,

They all walked off to the dining room and were all seated at the same table, the drinks waiter brought over their requested drinks and informed them that after the meal if they returned to their rooms and awaited the judges decisions, there would be of course another drink waiting for them in their rooms and then in the morning they would be taken to the presentation Hall where the ceremony would take place. They were all excited and enjoyed the meal and the company at around ten thirty they all retired to their rooms where as promised the drinks were waiting, they bid each other good night and wished each other good luck.

At midnight the Brotherhood made their move, Shaun was taken out through the fire door first, the alarm had been silenced after Jaymo had asked room service to leave it open so that he could go for a smoke without upsetting his wife, after slipping the guy twenty quid he was happy to oblige.

Once secured in the van Jaymo and A.J. went for Helen, she was easier as she didn't weigh as much as Shaun and it didn't take long to secure her after they got Simon they all went to the rooms and emptied them of all of their possessions so it looked like no-one had been there, Martin made sure that all the surfaces were wiped down with bleach cloths, after leaving the room and taking all of the rubbish with them he wiped the door handles and then slipped out the fire door with the other two, ensuring that it closed behind him.

In one hour they were in the hide out and bringing in the last of the three captives once everyone was secured Martin rang the house manager at the hotel and inform him that he was the head judge and they had decided that none of the candidates were worthy winners of any of the awards and he had asked them to leave and go home, which they had, this was just a courtesy call to say that the rooms were now available for other people to use and they would settle the bill tomorrow.

A.J. made sure that the three captives came round and that they were given fluids to ensure that the drug was diluted enough and able to come out of their systems, they wouldn't be released to go to the toilet they could do it were they hung, all three were shackled to the wall, gagged and hooded.

The following day the Hotel received the money for the rooms along with a thank you note from the Charity and could they please send the receipt to the P.O. Box mentioned in the note, they didn't need a receipt but it threw less suspicion on them if it all seemed legit.

"If you think we are going to let you go then you've got another think coming", said Martin,

Martin walked over to Simon and placed his head next to his hooded face, "Tell me something that I don't know", he said,

Simon whispered to him the name of the head man in the prison and how if there was any trouble they were to contact him and the code they were to use before speaking to him so that he knew that they were genuine. Martin stood back in disbelief at the news he had just been given, how could this be, the one man you would least suspect of any type of involvement in this sordid affair, but this man had just been named as one of the co-conspirators.

Martin looked at the other captives and wondered if this information could be verified by any of those two. He slowly moved the ten paces to where Shaun was shackled and then whispered in his ear. Shaun began to weep but through his sobs confirmed what Simon had told Martin, the only difference being the code that he used.

Martin looked down at the piece of paper he had in his hand, he had two codes so lets see if he could make it three, he moved to Helen and placed his mouth close to her hooded face,

"Tell me who your contact at the prison is?" he asked,

killed as well", what I want you two to do is act normal and go to work as usual but stay alert, because for all we know there could be others working within the establishment and we haven't uncovered them yet", stated Martin,

A.J. and Jaymo weren't happy with the situation but agreed; if no-one else was involved the safest place would be the Prison for all of them.

A.J. had produced a shift pattern for the three of them to take turns in ensuring that the captives were alive and fed, any problems they were to ring the other two before any one was untied or released for any reason, once they were all in attendance then they would decide on a plan of action.

One evening whilst Martin was doing his duty run of feeding and watering his guests, one of them decided that he had some information that he would like to share with him, Martin asked him to carry on as he was listening, but the captive, Simon wanted to be away from the other two, Martin declined his kind offer and then proceed to leave the room and as he opened the door Simon shouted,

"Wait I'll tell you the person who is in charge at the prison, that no-one suspects because of who he is",

"I'm waiting, but I'm not going to stand here much longer",

"If I tell you, what's in it for me?" he said,

Chapter 27

Their gags were removed but their hoods remained on, they were informed that they were being held captive because of who they were,

"Do you know who I work for, and I don't mean the Prison Service", Simon spat,

"Why do you think you are all here, numb nuts", said Jaymo,

"Your dead people", he replied,

"Don't threaten us, just remember you'll be dead well before we are, now listen you can scream and shout as much as you want no-one will hear you because your about twenty something feet underground and the walls in here are about two feet thick, so try and keep the screaming down to a minimum and make yourselves as comfortable as possible in the circumstances,"

Jaymo left turning off the light and closing the door behind him and then made sure that the electronic keypad lock was activated after that he made his way to the boardroom.

"What are we going to do with these three now that we have them?" said Jaymo,

"We will hold them hostage just in case something happens to any of us, I'm going to wire up the room with explosive so that if someone does attempt to get them out they will be

Jaymo had made sure that they had enough provisions for a long stay and to help mask the smell they had one of those spray packs which you attach to your back and fill with weed killer, but theirs was full of disinfectant this would be sprayed on the captives as well as the floor around their feet, Martin had moved all of the valuable merchandise and trinkets from the hide out and had asked Imee to remove them from the country and have them stored until he needed them. A.J. had gotten all the medical supplies and had set up a small table at one end of the room with all of his medicines etc on it, it looked like a field hospital and that he could if he wished carry out major surgery but he wouldn't.

She confirmed what the other two had said and the code she was to use," but also that she was sure that they knew nothing about any Brotherhood, because they would have eliminated all of you without giving it a second thought."

Simon shouted out for Martin to come to him as he had more information, Martin moved back,

"They do know about you, well not you exactly, they knew someone was messing in their business so they had him blown up, they thought it was just one nosey officer",

"Albear", whispered Martin,

He walked away from them and out of the room ensuring that he locked it securely behind him, as they all started shouting together asking to be set free,

"We have told you everything, please lets us go and you'll never hear from us again, we promise."

Martin could feel the anger welling up inside him as he walked into the store room and started to remove the explosives that he had stored in there two months ago, he opened the first box and pulled out a statue of Indra sat on an elephant. "How appropriate" thought Martin that he'd picked up the Hindu King of Gods or Devas and Lord of Heaven or Svargaloka in Hindu mythology, he is the God of War, Storms and Rainfall, and trust me there was going to be almighty War and the storm that that would bring, as the crap rained from above onto the those who perpetrated these crimes deserved everything that was coming their way.

Martin looked at the statue and muttered to himself,

"It's amazing what they can do with plastic explosive nowadays",

Martin recalled who he had got the explosives from, he had been talking to one of the cons within the prison who had been bragging that he could get anything so Martin called his bluff and challenged him to prove it, a few minutes later the con came back with a phone number,

"Ring this number and speak to Mo, ask for whatever you want and he will get it for you",

That night he made a phone call from a phone box and told the person answering that he had been given the number by an acquaintance and was told to ask for Mo,

"This is Mo",

Martin told him that he wanted some high grade plastic explosive, about four crates, Mo made a smart arse comment about starting world war three,

"Can you supply it?" said Martin,

"How do we do the hand over", asked Mo,

"I'll drop off the money at a site of my choosing and then you drop off the parcel, now set your price",

"Four boxes that will be five grand a box",

"Don't talk wet, two is the max that we are willing to go up to", said Martin,

"Two and a half and you can have it within two weeks and modelled so as not to raise suspicion as to what it really is", replied Mo,

"It's a deal I'll call you in two weeks and give you the drop off site, just to show trust, before delivery I will give you half up front, give me an address where you want the money dropping off".

Mo give him the address and sure enough one week later he received a phone call and he was told to go outside and pick his money up before someone passing by decided to take it and then the phone went dead, from the shadows Martin watched as Mo came to his front door and picked the money up.

Now he was moulding the explosive back into a more usable shape and smiling to himself, this is true justice using their own merchandise against them, after he had reshaped above thirty of these statues he took the rest down the tunnels a case at a time one case for each tunnel, that's what he had been told, he then returned to the store and took out the fuse wire, he was first going to go down each tunnel and lay the wires giving himself enough spare at each end to do with as he wished and as he came out of the tunnel he would secure the wire to the ceiling this was to ensure that the tunnel would collapse with the explosion when he got to the centre he left them as he was told, these would be later attached to a control box which would have a remote detonator, Martin took everything out of the room and distributed it around the hideout at different locations, he would return later.

He wondered what he should do with the information he had been given, should he share it with the others or keep it to himself and act on it alone so that no-one else could be linked to what he was planning for the leader and betrayer of men and women, this was a quandary that only he could decide upon, he locked everything up and walked down the church tunnel this was the closet to the car park and it also afforded you a view of the car park before exiting the tunnel, Martin checked it was all clear he left the tunnel and walked towards his car as he got closer he noticed a note under his windscreen wiper, he picked it up opened it and read it, he then took his pen from his top pocket wrote on it and then screwed it up into a ball and dropped it on the floor close by, he then got in his car a drove off without looking back.

The following day all was the same the Brotherhood all went back to work and carried on as if nothing had happened, there were a few rumours flying around the prison about three staff that had gone missing but they thought that two of them and run off together and the third had just left to live in Spain because he had had enough of working for the Prison Service, only three people knew the truth and they weren't saying anything.

Martin finished his early shift at twelve and drove off to the hide out; the others were on Main shifts and wouldn't be their till after five o'clock so Martin had time to himself.

As he entered the tunnel and went down the stairs he found a note pinned to the control box he read the note and put it in his pocket and went into the board room, everything here had to be cleared out and made sterile so Martin started the process the other two could assist him when they arrived, he looked around and imagined the history that was in this place and the Brothers who had come before him to champion the true just courses of their day and to right the wrongs that had been committed by evil and greedy individuals, he had nearly cleared all of the Board room when he got the phone call.

Chapter 28

A.J. had just finished his evening duty and was leaving the prison with the rest of his fellow officers as they came out of the gate lodge they all seemed to take a gulp of fresh air to rid themselves of the stench of the prison, this was a psychosomatic urge which never really removed any of the smell from their clothes or from their nostrils this was just a natural instinct and no-one noticed that they all tended to do this other than to two figures sat in a car watching them across the road from the jail, it had been a long day and all that A.J. wanted to do was to get home and get in bed.

A.J. hadn't noticed the officer behind him rushing through the others so that he could keep him in sight, the officer looked over to the main road and spotted what he was looking for, Ralph and Steve Manchester were sat smoking in their car, he attempted to get their attention without making it obvious to everyone else.

Lucky for him only the brothers noticed his feeble attempts to get their attention, they nodded at him to show a sign of recognition, using his eyes and head he pointed out A.J. to them, they acknowledged that they had seen him and they started their car in readiness. The officer then walked over to a group of officers that had stopped on the car park for a chat, this was so he could distance himself from the carnage that was about to befall A.J.

After throwing his bag into the back of the car he got in and started the engine, he tooted his horn and waved at his colleagues and then pulled out of the car park, he failed to notice the clapped out Volvo Estate parked on the main road that had just pulled out to following him. He continued up the main road and then turned into what was known as the Jewish quarter of Manchester, he still didn't notice the vehicle which by now was just a couple of car lengths behind him, but as he looked in his rear view mirror for the fourth time it began to dawn on him that he might be being followed but he still wasn't sure or was he just being paranoid. He decided to deviate from his normal route by taking a couple of turns down the streets just to make sure. He made a left turn and then a right, the car was still with him now he was sure that he was being followed. He was now back on the main road and began to speed up. He reached into his glove compartment for his mobile phone and as he hit the speed dial on his phone, he was rear ended by the Volvo with such force that he dropped the phone on the car floor as it continued to call, he looked up to see that the lorry in front had stopped, but he was now being pushed into its path and at some speed, he slammed his foot onto the brake, but to no avail it was too late, he hit the vehicle in front with such force that he was knocked unconscious.

Jaymo's mobile rang but when he picked it up and put it to his ear all he could hear was the crunching of metal, a scream and then an almighty thud, then silence,
"Hello" he shouted but there was no answer, nothing,
He checked the caller ID, it was A.J. so he started shouting his name and then listening intently for any hint as to what had happened, that's when he heard the other voices,
"Paul, grab him and throw him into the van, before the cops turn up", he heard one of the voices say.
Jaymo could hear a siren in the background it was getting closer, that's when he heard the vehicle race off with its wheels screeching, then nothing just the sound of the siren which suddenly blasted his ears off, it must have pulled up right next to A.J.'s car, then the siren stopped altogether.

He could hear the Policeman's radio they wanted an update of the situation, the officer answered it and said,
"Victor Charlie two four log me as on scene at cross roads of Half way house in Higher Broughton, I currently have two abandoned vehicles and a lorry driver, request medical assistance and also another Traffic Unit so as to assist with

the collation of witness statements, two recovery vehicles and to help get this lot moving again, VC 24 out."

Jaymo got into his car which was on the Prison car park, that's not far from here it shouldn't take me too long he thought, he pulled off the car park at brake neck speed and headed for the accident scene, as he got closer the traffic started getting heavier so he pulled over and parked his car in a side street. He put on his coat on over the top of his uniform to conceal the fact that he was a prison officer and then walked the rest of the way. When he got there he got his mobile out and rang Martin and told him what had happened and that he was now at the scene and A.J was nowhere to be seen. He described the scene to Martin , "there was an ambulance crew wondering around aimlessly looking for a casualty and a Policeman was now taking statements off the people who were stood around," Jaymo walked around the crowd which had grown and stopped next to one of the eye witnesses who was now giving a statement to the Policeman. He held his phone to his side so Martin could hear.

"These guy's just rammed that car (pointing to A.J.'s car) into that lorry, the driver seemed to be unconscious and I thought the two guys behind who had caused the accident where going to help him, but they just pulled him out of the car and then this black van turned up from nowhere and they chucked the driver into it and then sped off towards the Hospital but I don't think they took him there because you can see the turning for the Hospital from here and they never turned right at those lights down there", the witness pointed down the road at the Hospital turning.

"Where did they go, could you see?"
"No", said the witness," They went straight through the lights and just kept going",
"Did you manage to see the registration number of the black van?"
"No, it happened so quickly, and as I said, I thought that they were going to help the driver not kidnap him".
"Thank you" said the Police man, "We will be in touch if we need anything else, you've been a great help".
Jaymo lifted his mobile to his ear,
"What should we do", he said,
"Come to the hide out, but be careful, make sure your not being followed", said Martin.
Jaymo hung up and looked around at the scene trying to take in every detail of what beheld him so that he could tell Martin, the ambulance crew were still wondered around looking everywhere for someone to treat, the Policeman was

now eying up the crushed vehicles wondering why the hell anyone would leave this scene as they did and a lorry driver was stood next to the Policeman badgering him as to where the heck the drivers had gone and who was he going to pay for the damage to his vehicle, because his boss wasn't going to pay and it wasn't coming out of his wages, Jaymo slowly walked back to his car still trying to figure out why anyone would what to do this to A.J.

When he got back to his car there was a note under his windscreen wiper,

"Shit booked for parking on yellow lines, but there were no yellow lines", he picked up the note and read it,

"Your being followed, two men in a green Vauxhall currently parked by the park",

Jaymo slowly moved his head so as to be able to see the car, it didn't take him long as he glanced in their direction the two of them looked away,

he quickly put the note into his pocket and looked around seeing if anyone was else was watching him, he never noticed the dark figure hiding in a gate way in the alleyway just off to the side of him, Jaymo got into his car and locked the doors, still looking around he started his car and slowly pulled back into the traffic which was now running a lot more easily, the two in the car started off just four cars behind, when Jaymo got to the Policeman he stopped and said something to the Policeman who looked up and stared straight at the two in the green car, when the two saw this they turned into the first street and made off, the Policeman got onto his radio and gave the number plate of the car and the make and model, the mysterious figure came out from his hiding place and began to walk off down the street.

The next thing A.J. felt was someone's hand slapping him with a great deal of vigour, as he came round and tried to move he realised that his legs and arms were strapped down to a solid wooden chair and that his hands, arms and legs were being held in place by leather straps, everything started to come into focus and he began looking around, he was in a room with nothing but a table chair and a bloody bright light that was hurting his eyes, he was slapped again, "Stop it I'm awake now what the hell is going on", he said,
He noticed now that the leather straps had metal studs and wing nuts attached to them and then some kind of wire leading off behind him, he tried to move his head but that had been held by a strap to his forehead,
"Thank goodness", came the reply, "You sure took your sweet time coming round",

A.J. looked towards to direction of the voice and then he came into focus the guy had his back to him he was stood next to a small table to his right and on it was what looked like a doctors bag the man was taking medical instruments out of the bag and placing them on the table.

"Its ok I'm not that badly injured if you just undo these bindings I will stand up and show you, I'm just a bit groggy", said A.J.,

The man turned around and that's when the penny dropped for A.J. because he recognised the man, it was Ralph Manchester and he also knew what Ralph was renowned for, and that was being a sadistic and cruel individual and he was going to be on the receiving end of a lot of pain, but why?.

"What do you want?" said A.J

"Answers to some questions, and we think that you will know these answers, so the quicker you answer those questions the less pain you will receive, but just to show you that we mean business, I'm going to give you a taste of what you will get if I think your either lying or that I think your holding back",

Ralph walked over to A.J. all the time A.J. was searching with his eyes as to what he had in his hand, but he couldn't see due to his head being restrained, well not until he felt the excruciating pain running through his body. Every muscle in his body seemed to cease up and he thought he was going to bite his tongue off, and then it stopped,

"Now", said Ralph, "Tell me about the brotherhood",

"Who?" and before he could say anything else his whole body was reeling in agonising pain, the pain stopped just as suddenly as it had started,

"Let me say it again shall I", said Ralph,

"Tell me about the brotherhood",

Chapter 29

Jaymo made it to the hideout in quick time just hoping that he hadn't got caught by any speed cameras, he jumped out in the car park and walked over to the ticket machine and put his money in, as he turned round he was startled to see Martin right behind him,

"What the! said Jaymo,

"Anyone follow you"?

"No!"Two guys tried but with a little help from the boys in blue he scared them off and I haven't seen them since, now what the hells going on?"

"We have to act quickly, one of the gangs has A.J. and it's not going to be long before they will be coming for us so we have to plan what we are going to do, come with me",

Martin rushed off to the hideout and the two of them disappeared into the depth of the earth, as they descended it became really quite and eerie the two of them never spoke until they entered the meeting room, the place looked massive without the rest of the Brotherhood, the two of them walked over to the white board that Jaymo had put all of the pictures of the gang members on, as he looked at it Martin and was just about to start going though the details of each gang starting with the Manx, when Jaymo realised that he still had his car park ticket in his hand and that he had left his car open,

"I'll be back in a jiffy" he said,

Of he went up through the nearest exit and then onto the car park, as he reached his car he felt something cold and hard in his back,

"Move and I'll kill you were you stand, just give us a reason to kill you please", said the stranger,

"I won't move I'm not armed, what do you two want",

Just then there was a thud and Jaymo felt water on the left side of his face and on the back of his neck, then there was another thud and he felt water on the right side of his face and more water on his neck, the two men then both pushed him forward one after the other,

"Alright I'll move no need to push just tell me where you want me to go", as he moved forward he felt the two of them slide down his back, which made his legs buckle which caused him to stumble forward,

"Where do you want me to go"? There was no response so Jaymo looked round and saw that the two men had been shot in the head, and there was blood and brain oozing out of holes.

"What the" he whispered

Jaymo took cover behind a car and scanned the area high and low looking for the killer he couldn't see anyone and then it occurred to him, why in God's name was he hiding the guy had just saved his life by shooting the men who had shoved a pistol into his back and were going to kill him, Jaymo stood up and quickly placed the ticket in his car window and then made his way to the hide out watching for anyone or anything out of the ordinary, he made it to the opening and then began to descend the stairs three at a time tripping up for the last few, Martin came out to see what the commotion was, Jaymo was on the floor and Martin could see the blood on the back of his neck,

"Christ what the hell happened, Are you ok?"

Jaymo looked up from the floor trying to catch his breath, Martin bent down to help him up,

"They knew I was here and they were waiting for me by my car, they were going to kill me, but someone shot them,"

"Who shot who; you're not making any sense,"

Martin helped him up and took him into the meeting room and sat him down, he poured him a drink and told him to take small sips and try and calm down, Martin walked over to the table and took some wipes and began to remove the blood from his neck and back,

"Stop", said Jaymo, "They know we are here they must have followed me from the crash scene but I didn't see them, I'm sorry",

"Don't worry; just tell me whose blood it is",

Jaymo told him what happened and that he thought he was going to die when out of the blue someone shot these the two goons who had pulled a gun on him, but that he couldn't see who had done it, so he ran back to the hideout to warn Martin.

By now the Police armed response team had arrived on the scene and contained the area, they had set up a cordon around the car park and the hideout, Martin had taken a look through the spy holes grateful that they were there as they didn't compromise their safety and then went back down, when he entered the room Jaymo had calmed down and was feeling a lot better.

"We will have to stay here tonight so ring your wife and make your excuses because the Police have blocked the whole place off, we could be here for a while, just tell her to start packing and you'll see her in a few days", Jaymo did as he was told and Martin did the same, they also rang work to book off sick for a few days.

Martin went into the other room and rang Imee, he would have to make arrangements quicker than he had expected but if anyone could do it Imee was your man. After an hour or so later Martin went back to the meeting room, Jaymo had just finished talking to his wife whilst at the same time removing the rest of the blood off his face and chest, he had changed into the work clothes that he had left down there and now looked a lot more presentable and not like an extra from the living dead,

"How you feeling", said Martin

"Much better and things are a lot clearer now but I still cannot figure out who did the shooting and why",

"Just count you're blessings", said Martin,

"Yeah",

The two men then turned their attention to the white board, someone on here is calling all the shots but who and what was their game plan?

Chapter 30

A.J. tried to shake off the effects of the last electric shocks that had been inflicted on his body but to no avail as soon as he seemed to feel some kind of normality in his body, Ralph would ask him again and again giving him shock after shock at one stage A.J. felt the blood coming from his mouth running down his chin, he spat it out towards Ralph, he had bit his tongue and could feel a small piece of it swilling around in the blood in his mouth,

"You bastard stop",

To A.J.'s. surprise Ralph did and then slowly walked back to his operating table and placed the electrodes onto it, someone else was in the room, A.J. couldn't see him yet but he heard the door bang shut and could make out a shadow coming towards Ralph.

"Strewth Ralph do you have to make such a mess, looks like he's bitten his tongue off, he hasn't has he",

"No he hasn't, what do you want?" he sneered

A.J. moved his head and looked towards where the voice was coming from, he could just see the other person it was Steve Manchester.

AJ noticed he was immaculately dressed in a pin stripped suit white shirt and a pinstriped tie and patent leather winkle picker shoes, as he was still walking towards A.J. wincing and grimacing at the state of the injuries that had been inflicted by his brother on this poor sole in front of him.

"Don't get too close, not in those clothes not unless you mind them getting covered in blood",

"These cost an arm and a leg, don't you dare get blood on them", he said

Just then A.J. gave an almighty blast of blood from his mouth which covered Steve's new togs,

"YOU", he spat, Steve tensed every muscle in his body, he was angry,

He turned and with all of might he hit A.J. full on in the face bursting his nose into his face and smashing one of his eye sockets, he continued to hit him until his brother stepped in and stopped him, Steve looked at his brother with his nostrils flaring and with the look of a man possessed by the devil, he had hit A.J. with such force he broke the strap holding his head still.

"Stop we need to get information from him and if you kill him we will be back at square one", said Ralph,

Steve moved back and then stormed out of the room slamming the door behind him cursing.

A.J.'s head was slumped forward and there was blood coming from most of his facial orifices and he seemed to be unconscious, Ralph lifted his head to look at the wounds and decided that he would leave him for tonight and would begin again tomorrow, he threw a small damp cloth over his head and walked towards the exit, he slammed the door behind him and locked it. After a while A.J. slowly began to move his head up and using his one good eye scanned the room to make sure he was alone. He was and he now had a better view of the whole room, there was a large window which was behind him and he could make out that there was a hill in the distance with trees on it but it was about half a mile away too far for him to run to and get cover before being gunned down, at least his mind was still working he thought as he started to try and remove the leather strapping from his wrists and arms using his teeth.

After releasing one arm he then found it more easy to undo the rest, he was still weak from the electric shock treatment and was unsteady on his feet, he managed to walk over to a sink in the corner of the room and with the cloth he washed the blood from his face and washed out the taste of blood from his mouth, whilst swilling his mouth he spat out a tooth A.J. tried to stop it going down the plug hole but failed miserable and as it tinkled down the drain he heard someone coming, he moved as fast as he could to find something from the tools of Ralphs trade to protect himself with, looking at the table he picked up a hammer and a scalpel and then went to the door and waited.

The door opened up slowly and as A.J. was about to strike, the door hit him with such force that it knocked him down, he scrambled to his feet and stood in the middle of the room with both weapons out ready, Ralph entered the room and slammed the door behind him.

"This is going to be the unluckiest day of your miserable life", he said,

"I'm going to give you so much pain that you will be begging me to end it and just kill you, but I won't, I'm going to make you suffer and then I'm going after your friends and family",

A.J.'s. eyes started to fill up and he could feel that this was going to be a do or die situation, he began to slowly step backwards towards the large window still keeping his eyes on Ralph just hoping for some kind of miracle to happen, just then the window behind him popped, he turned around to see a perfect round circle in the middle of the glass, remembering who was now behind him he spring around only to see Ralph stood there rigid and with a look of surprise on his face, that's when A.J. noticed the small hole in his head which had some blood coming from it.

Ralph hit the floor face first without flinching, A.J. turned back around and glanced out of the window and saw something on the hill glisten, after that he didn't wait he moved as quickly and quietly as possible making sure that no-one else heard or saw him. Once outside he made for the hill towards were he had seen something glistening as he made his way up and out of sight he heard the racket coming from the factory behind him,

"They must have discovered Ralph's body and would be after him soon",

A.J. ran for his life not knowing what or who his was going to find at the top of the hill all he knew was if this person was going to kill him they could have done it in the factory along with Ralph Manchester, just as he reached the hills brow he felt the bang to the back of his head and it all went dark.

Chapter 31

Jaymo was at his wits end he had seen the majority of his friends die for a cause that he was now believing was a price too high for him to pay, he wanted to live to a ripe old age with his wife and family, not end up either holding up a bridge on the M62, dead in some dirty rat infested alleyway or blown to bits with his family like Albear was. Enough was enough, Jaymo rang Genghis, Steve Manchester and Tyrone and requested a meeting with all of them, he explained to them that he was one of a band of brothers who had made it their mission to eliminate the officers who were in their gangs and also employed by the Prison Service and to eliminate their bosses and their brothers. Initially he was met with a torrid of abuse and threats but after letting them calm down they all agreed to meet him in a mutually agreeable place, somewhere which afforded them all the security of not being over heard and also were Jaymo could feel safe from being killed, they decided on the Trafford Centre, one because communications with in this building could be blocked by use of a high powered signal blocker and each gang leader could also have eyes on the top floor whilst the meeting was taking place in the dining area in front of the big screen, Jaymo had previously reconnoitred the area and had taped off an area in the dining area, using the Trafford security's own tape so that no-one working their would be suspicious.

All of the remaining gang members had agreed to call a truce just until they had rid themselves of these tiresome and annoying individuals once and for all, they would pay dearly for the deaths of the gangs members and those who would make sure were Paul's remaining brother Steve, Ranjit's right hand man Genghis and Marvin's henchman Tyrone along with the remnants of what was left of all three gangs after it had been trimmed down by the brotherhood. Unbeknown to Jaymo they had also agreed that after they had killed the so called leader of this group, Jaymo was next as he would have out lived his usefulness but until then, they had an ace up their sleeve; Jaymo had turned on Martin and had set him up for the ultimate penalty, death.

After Jaymo had switched off his blocker he phoned Martin and asked him to meet him at the hideout at three o'clock the following day which he had agreed to, this was overheard by the gang leaders whilst they sat in the Trafford centre with him.

Jaymo took the gang down to the hideout and into the boardroom, as they sat there waiting they became bored and decided to have a look around, when they came across the room with the electronic key pad lock, Tyrone began punching random numbers to see if he could open it, it didn't, when Jaymo spotted them he walked over and asked Tyrone to move and he would open it for them, he punched in the access code and when he opened the door Tyrone spotted the three officers who were in some distress, they had been tied up to the far wall and they looked like crosses on the whitewashed wall, everyone rushed in to see the sight for themselves and then it suddenly dawned on them that these three were their officers they could see that they were gagged but with their eyes and heads they seemed to be trying to tell them something as the got closer it was Genghis who was the first to spot what they were trying to point to, it was a statue of Indra and it had wires leading from it, that's when he realised what it was, he turned to the others and screamed for them to get out, but it was too late the door behind them had been shut and locked by Jaymo who was now nowhere to be seen, Genghis turned back around with the look of realisation of what was to come.

All of a sudden there was a brilliant flash of light that lasted for about three minutes after which there was a whooshing sound and then the whole place blew up with an almighty bang and the whole of Bury shook, after all the dust had settled where once was a spectacular monument there was now a massive crater, the electric cables were sparking, the water pipes had burst and water was gushing all down the street and the gas main had broken and was on fire.

It resembled a film scene from the blitz, within minutes the Police, Fire service and ambulance crews were on the scene to assess the situation and try and figure out what had happened.

"Looks like a gas main has blown" said the Fire Chief,

"We have multiple fatalities, ten so far we think, there's body parts everywhere and we also have a few walking wounded, were going to need some more body bags" said the ambulance man,

"We have cordoned off the area and the gas board are on their way" said the Police Inspector,

Overhead at about twenty thousand feet Martin and his family were sat on a jumbo jet heading for America, Martin looked at his watch, it was 3 o'clock he turned to the window and breathed a sigh of relief,

He turned and looked at his wife and smiled, they were off to start afresh.

hree months back Martin had had a secret meeting with Imee and asked him to purchase a business in the small town of Mount Dora in Florida, Imee brought two orange working relationship had now removed themselves from the equation permanently.

The phone rang and as he picked it up the door burst open and in walked two MI5 agents the first one walked up to the Governor and placed his hand on his shoulder and said,

"Your under arrest, you do not have to say anything, but it may harm your defence if you do not mention when questioned something which you later rely on in court, anything you do say may be given in evidence, do you understand what I have just explained to you",

"Yes", said the Governor.

The MI5 agent took the phone off the Governor as the other one placed the handcuffs on him,

"We have him", said the agent to the person on the other end of the phone,

"Thank you", then it went dead,

Martin replaced the receiver onto the phone and smiled; now we have them all he thought to himself.

Martin drifted back to the time he was in the hide out with the three bogus officers and they all confirmed that the Governing Governor of HMP Patricroft was their main man in the prison and after telling him the code the Governor had confirmed that all was well and they could continue as before.

blue light straight away; Marvin was still alive, well just barely.

Monday morning the Governing Governor of the Prison was handed his mail by his secretary and as she did so she said, "There are a few from officers requesting that you accept their letters as their formal resignation from the Prison Service",

The Governor looked at her bemused, "Who?"

"I'll let you have that little surprise" she said, and then closed the office door,

He began to sift through the mail, and as he opened the letters he began to smile and as he went through them his smile became bigger and bigger until finally he said to himself, "Good luck guys, you deserve it"

There was a knock at his door and then the door opened, it was his secretary, and this time she had a parcel,

"This has just been delivered, it's been x-rayed, and it's uniform."

The Governor smiled as he took it from her and she left the room, he placed it on his desk and was about to pick the phone up and dial a number, he would have to ring three different numbers to inform these people that all was well and that they could now continue their business uninterrupted as the individuals who were destroying their

Chapter 32

Paul Manchester was found hanging in his cell later that weekend as all the other prisoners were in their cells watching yet another Manchester derby between City and United, every time a goal was scored the prisoners would bang on the cell doors which made an almighty din, all the old officers knew what was coming and would smile as they watched the looks on the faces of the new officers, who would shit themselves every time the banging started, it sounded like a riot was about to happen. The wing Senior Officers reported the death to the Duty Governor who ordered the wing locked down and a full head count done to ensure that all the other prisoners were ok and that none of them had followed Pauls lead, as the officers went round they discovered Ranjit Ali and Marvin Johnstone in the shower recess together, Ranjit had been strangled to death and Marvin had been stabbed twice in the stomach and was bleeding profusely. The security department and the Duty Governor were informed and the Senior Officer set up a cordon so that the crime scene would remain intact, he got one of his officers to start a log of everyone going in and out of the area, he told him not to leave anyone out as this could be used in a court case. The medics arrived and requested a groves along with a packing factory which he had had up dated and modernised all at cost of course, along with this he had purchased three properties for rental so that Martin and his family would have an income and a legitimate right to remain in America for as long as they wished, Martin had brought a small holding on the edge of Lake Beauclar this property had a couple of acres of land, out houses and a stable, along with a boat which was moored on the jetty.

Martin had taken this information to Imee who had passed it on to his MI5 mates and they had investigated the Governor and his association with these gangs.

Chapter 33

Everything was so tranquil and life was good, all of their troubles were now behind them and after a few months they had forgotten about the brotherhood and HMP Patricroft.

One morning as Martin and Ann sat on the veranda having breakfast, drinking coffee and looking out at the lake watching the birds skimming the water searching for fish, their peace was disturbed by a noise to their right, the two of them turned towards the driveway as they had both heard a car coming up the gravel driveway, Ann instinctively knew what to do, she got up from the table and went into the house and headed towards the kitchen, Martin stood up as the car came to a halt and the two people inside alighted from the vehicle and walked towards Martin, as they reached the bottom step of the veranda Ann came from the house with two cups in her hands, Martin opened up his arms to welcomed his guests.

"Jaymo, Margret welcome to our humble abode how are you two settling in",

"Everything is great, ours is the mirror image of your place, you can just see it if you stand this end of your veranda", said Jaymo.

The two men embraced each other again, and then Martin took Jaymo to one side and said,

"I need to know, what happened at the hideout," did everything go according to our plan."

"Well after they saw the three officers tied to the far wall they all dived into the room, that gave me time to get into the secret exit at the side of the room and ran like hell knowing that I only had a few minutes to get out of reach of the blast, after shutting them in I made my way to the secret passage going as fast as my feet would carry me, the next thing I remember is coming too in the Church yard just in time to see the whole place blow, there must have been some kind of delay thank God because I would have been a goner if it had set off when it was supposed to have done, anyway it was horrendous the whole ground shook and people were screaming as bits of gang members and debris came falling from the sky it was raining body parts and earth, the National press has put it down as gang warfare, a fight for overall rule of the Greater Manchester area and are asking what the Police intend to do about this unacceptable crime wave which is embroiling innocent people," the two of them laughed out loud and shook hands.

Just then Ann and Margret shouted together we have company coming, it's the Police, that's when they both turned and looked as the siren got louder and louder they looked up towards the driveway entrance they could see the Sheriff's vehicle, it screamed to a halt blowing up a cloud of smoke, the Sheriff jumped out of his car.

"For Christ sake Daz slow it down, you're supposed to be upholding the law not breaking it",

Jaymo started laughing and pointed at Daz,

"What the hell is going on",

He looked at Martin for an answer,

Martin nodded towards Daz and then said, "He was your delay and also the one who pulled you out of the shit, and apparently you hit your head,"

Daz walked up the stairs towards the stunned Jaymo,

"Sorry mate, if we hadn't kept it secret more of us would have died, I delayed the explosion so you would think that everything had gone to plan except for a little bit of a hiccup but you witnessed the ending as I did and besides with your clumsy feet it's a good job I did control the timing device, how's your head",

Jaymo rubbed his head where he had fallen in the tunnel,

"We had to let everyone think that Daz was died so that he could operate undercover otherwise none of us would have been getting out of there alive, we set up the pictures, we used loads of porridge oats and food colouring to make it look like concrete but this was purely in the belief that Daz would be able to find out who were the main players and take care of them so to speak and at the same time try and ensure that we stayed alive as long as possible, the only thing was whilst looking out for me and you they took A.J. and tortured him so as to find out about us and where we were."

Daz did find out who had him and made sure that they paid for their mistake in torturing one of us, and besides, "you didn't think that I was going to lay all of those explosives did you; you would have died along with everyone else, and as for the Sheriff here, Daz has always wanted to be the Sheriff of a small town and there was a vacancy so he filled it, by the way he lives just up from you to your right with his new wife, she's American it helped with his application to become the Sheriff, but this was only after ensuring that we got away safely."

Jaymo and Daz gave each other a hug and Jaymo said,

"I'm glad you're still alive it's just a shame that we couldn't save the others as well",

Just then the passenger door swung open and slowly but surely the other person alighted the vehicle,

"Sheriff you're a maniac if you don't slow down I'll be doing an autopsy on you and I can tell you now that the cause of death will be your own stupidity", said the Doc,

"Leave it out Doc, your just scared of any kind of speed", said Daz,

Jaymo looked toward the person they addressed as Doc,

"A.J." he screamed,

"Doc if you don't mind," said A.J.

A.J. had finally finished his Medical degree and was now employed as the towns Doctor and Coroner,

"But what about John, he thinks that you are dead",

"And that's as it should be for his own safety, he knows nothing let him get on with his own life now" said A.J.,

All four men stood on the veranda and with cups in hand, Martin gave a toast to absent friends and they all clinked their cups together and said in unison,

"TO ABSENT FRIENDS GOD BLESS THEM AND LOOK AFTER THEM",

Chapter 34

The doorbell rang and a young man answered the door, it was a Fedex delivery man,

"Parcel for Mr",

"Right ", said the young man,

The delivery man handed over the parcel and asked the man to sign for it, which he did,

"Thank you, have a nice day", said the Fedex man as he walked away.

The young man walked into the house and then opened the door to the cellar, he turned on the light and went down the steps, at the bottom of the steps he walked to the far wall and turned the coat hanger on the wall to the right, suddenly the wall moved to the right opening up an entrance to a secret part of the house.

As he walked into the open area he closed the entrance behind him, secreting himself from the outside world, there were four anti chambers within this chamber each holding a different secret, he entered the first room which housed all of his electronic communication systems, computers, telephone, flat screen TV and DVD and video player along with an assortment of other items all used to assist him in his work.

He opened the package and took out the DVD and the diary, he placed the DVD into the player and started it, and at the same time he removed two letters and opened the one addressed to him he looked at the other which was addressed to some solicitors firm.

John a voice on the DVD said,

He looked up to see his best friend and his adopted Uncle A.J. a few tears welled up in eyes as he gazed upon the only person he loved other than his family who were dead, this man had saved him from self destruction and helped him make something of himself, his gaze softened as he looked and listened to his mentor, wondering why he would send him a DVD when every Friday these two went out to watch a movie and then have a meal before finally going home for a drink.

"John, please don't be angry but if you are watching this then I'm dead",

John jumped up to his feet knocking everything to the floor and then he let out this almighty scream,

"NO, NO, NO"!

He could scream as loud as he wanted, the place was sound proof, no-one would hear him, he eventually fell to the floor holding his head in his hands, how could this be happening again to him he thought and then began to sob uncontrollably, at twenty four he had lost his family and his best friend, after about an hour he sat down and watched the DVD from the beginning.

A.J. explained everything to him all about the Brotherhood of the Maahes and how he and his father were members of the fine and honourable group of men, but for his own protection and that of the brotherhood he would not name the rest of the group except to say that they were all upstanding members of the public.

He also wanted him to keep the diary and the gold box safe in their hideaway which the two of them had built as one day someone would come to reclaim what belong to the brothers and until that day he was to lead a fruitful life and find a young lady and settle down.

John still lived in the house his parents had left him in their will, but he had carried out a few modifications to the property as such the cellar had purpose built secret rooms and within one of these rooms he had built a shrine and alter, and this was the resting place of the gold box given to him by his fathers friend and his adopted uncle A.J. along with the box he had also been given a diary, unbeknown to him it was the diary of the brotherhood of the Maahes……